GW00360267

Fallen A

By

Elaine Sturgess

First published July 2017

978-0-9957210-5-0/ Fallen Angel / Paperback Edition

Published by Raise A Laugh Publishing. For more information visit www.raisealaugh.com or email: happy@raisealaugh.com

Cover model: Kady Knight, www.kadyknight.co.uk
Photography & Design: Marta Gillner, shineonphotography.co.uk

WARNING: FALLEN ANGEL CONTAINS SPOILERS!!!

Lisa Danforth is one of the main characters in my novel Gin And It, this is her story. If you find yourself engaging with her, you might, by Chapter 3, want to consider whether you might enjoy reading Gin And It first!

Gin And It is available in eBook and Paperback format from Amazon stores Worldwide.

About Gin And It

When Rachel and Frankie move to an idyllic but remote country village, they expect to be the subject of local gossip - and are fully prepared to be regarded as outsiders. But as they settle into their new home, they quickly find their shock value pales into insignificance when the underbelly of village life starts to reveal itself.

A series of bizarre events raise questions that beg for answers: What do the goat-keeping vicar and the postmistress do in the field opposite first thing every morning? How come the church is permanently closed? What's behind the village's pride in its two prostitutes (one for locals, one for incomers)? Why did the previous owner keep his cock in the pantry? And what is this mysterious "Club" everyone refers to?

As the intrigue builds, Rachel is determined to uncover the truth - and finds herself caught in a web of sex, lies and sellotape that tests her relationship and tears at the net curtain fabric of village life.

Foreword

Thank you, as always, to my family and friends for all your love and support. Special thanks to Tina and Kady Knight for such kindness and the incredible things you have done to help me promote Gin And It and Fallen Angel and raise funds for Cancer Care in Maria's memory. To Kady also for bringing Lisa to life so perfectly on the front cover. Thanks also to Marta Gillner of Shine On Photography for your amazing pictures and design.

To Anna, you are my Angel and my inspiration. T'estimo!

This book is dedicated to the memory of my beloved Maria.
With Love Always.

IV

Chapter 1

"Whipped cream and vodka…"

Lisa kneeled back on the bed and sighed. "I'm guessing you've got that with you?"

He nodded, his eyebrow raised.

Lisa sighed again. "Ok, tell me how."

"I'll put the whipped cream on. You take the vodka shot, but don't swallow. Hold it and put your mouth round the whipped cream."

The excitement in his voice made her want to wretch. She shifted slightly from her position straddling Doug's mammoth hairy body, her slight frame pale against his swarthy farmer's tanned legs. The thought fleetingly passed through her head that the delicacy of her light pink exotic bra and panty set seemed wasted on the rough needs of this giant Neanderthal. She looked down, grateful at least that there was one thing that wasn't giant as she contemplated her issue with lactose intolerance. She rapidly assessed the situation. It was going to be a pretty small portion of cream given what she was looking at. She nodded. There was no way that it was going to be too much to handle on something that insignificant. "Alright. Thirty quid extra. You need to pay Theresa."

He scowled. "But I paid for the cream and vodka in the shop!" He reached his hand behind his head, flicking up the bottom of the daisy spattered curtain to pull a paper bag from the window sill. He took out its contents and held the pot of Extra Thick towards her to prove his protest was legitimate.

"Oh for fucks sake!" Lisa threw her hands up in exasperation and climbed off his supine torso, grabbing at the clothes that she'd tossed carelessly on the floor by the side of the bed.

"What?" Doug propped himself up on his elbow and examined the cream, confused.

"You bought a pot that's on offer because it's at its sell by date?" Lisa grabbed the tub and stared at the bright yellow 'Reduced for quick sale' price label. She tapped it to make her point and thrust it back at him.

"Yeah, but it's only yesterday and I kept it in the fridge on low temperature. Here, look, I'll try it first." Doug scooped a dollop of the

1

cream on his finger and put it in his mouth.

Lisa watched him as his lip curled involuntarily. "You fucker! It's off! That cream's off!"

He looked at her, trying to remove the grimace from his face, but failing. She watched his mind running through it as his face betrayed his perplexed thoughts. "Well what's wrong with that effin' fridge then," he mumbled as he stared into the pot, "it should have been alright, it's only a day… or maybe I forgot to pay the electricity bill…" his voice trailed off and he involuntarily lowered the pot to cover himself and his shrinking desire.

Lisa put her arm into the sleeve of her crumpled white shirt. "Forget it. There's no money that would even begin to persuade me."

"Sorry." Doug looked dejected.

Lisa snatched his card off the cheap formica nightstand by the bed and pulled a pen from the top of her bag on the chair by its side. She put an angry tick against the 'Tuesday' box.

"No wait…" he stretched his hairy arm over and tried to grab the pen off her, but the mark was already made.

She jabbed her finger at him. "You pull that kind of trick again and I'll have you banned!" She narrowed her eyes and stared at him defiantly.

His eyes lost their steely stare and he relented, "Alright, fair enough, my mistake. Just, well, wanted somethin' a bit different."

Lisa huffed, "cheapskate" she threw at him as she tossed the card in his face, "you'll have to ask Sue now. I'm done with you."

"Nooo, no don't be like that…"

"Yes! That's it! Enough. If you want your quota, you'll have to see Sue. No more from me. I have to have some self respect!"

Doug sighed as he watched her pull on her skinny jeans and converse, "can we at least…"

"No!!! Nothing. Not. A. Thing." Lisa jabbed her finger at him again, getting into her angry stride now

"But I didn't even say wha…"

"It doesn't matter!" Lisa's voice rose to a shriek, "I don't fucking care what you were going to say. Whatever it is, the answer is NO!" Lisa glared at him as she grabbed her jacket. She stopped and stared at him, seething, wanting to release some more of the boiling rage that was welling up inside her. "And that's not even fucking Smirnoff!"

Doug looked at the half bottle of supermarket brand vodka that was lying by the pillow, bewildered by her fury.

"I deserve fucking Smirnoff you bastard!"

Lisa's lip curled in an expression of disgust and she glowered at him, "I'm out of here!"

Doug, seldom short of a word, was temporarily dumbstruck. All he could do was watch, his mouth gaping, as Lisa put the strap of her bag over her shoulder and strode to the door, turning and throwing one last glare at him before slamming it shut behind her.

"Jesus Christ! What the bloody blazes was all that about?" He stroked his beard and shook his shaggy head in disbelief as he picked up the pot of cream and stared at it. He sighed deeply as he looked at the offending yellow sticker. "Thirty-seven pence. Fuck it. What a waste."

Chapter 2

Lisa wiped at the tears that streamed down her face as she walked up the narrow alleyway by the side of the Cotswold stone cottage that had become her prison by day. As she brushed past the falling wisteria, it's beauty seemed incongruent with the tawdry secrets it veiled within the four walls that supported its growth. She scrambled in her bag and found a tattered tissue. She looked it and laughed at its lack of substance. Dabbing it under her nose, she knew it had no chance of performing its purpose in its pathetic state. She threw it irritatedly onto the ground and resorted to the back of her hand, grimacing as she felt the snot slime across her skin. "Ugh. Nothing ever works for me." The sad state of the tissue prompted a stronger flow of tears and she laughed harder through them at the fact that she was making matters worse. She stopped and looked back at the piece of white flimsy paper and, tutting, walked back, snatching it up and stuffing it into her handbag. She shook her head and berated herself for the fact that she couldn't even muster enough rebellious strength to leave a piece of litter on the ground. Exiting the narrow pathway, she stopped and stood still, looking up at the darkening midnight blue of the sky and the soft glow of the full moon as it shone above the church spire. She checked her watch. Nine-thirty. She hesitated, knowing she would be late if she didn't hurry and dreading the questioning of her Mother. "Fuck it. And fuck her," she mumbled as she made a determined decision to head to the park and its quiet sanctuary. Crossing the road, she glanced up at the camera that sat on the head of a particularly ugly gargoyle on the church's facade and smiled as it whirred into action and turned its beady glass eye towards her, following her past the church door and into the grave yard. She flicked the V's with her fingers and laughed. A small attempt at dissention, but nevertheless it made her feel good. She picked up her pace as she passed knowledgeably through the meandering pathway, occasionally touching one of the ancient leaning grave stones that bordered the narrow graveled track. She felt comfortable here amongst the stone memories of past lives. The tears dried and her mood started to lift. She smiled again as she saw the park and her favourite swing hanging idly on its silver metal chain, a shiny linked pendulum that she had used to rock and soothe herself for more years than she could remember. She put her hand on the cold steel and felt her body relax. "Hello…" she said quietly as she sat on the weathered smooth wood of the seat, which seemed somehow to be a perfect fit for her. She bent her knees and hooked her feet beneath her, stretching back to push the seat behind and then, letting go, released herself into the swing and stretched her legs out in front of her. As she rocked back and forth, building height, she felt the air swoosh around her and the rhythm filled her with the familiar flood of comfort. She let her breath out in a long flow that felt like peace and closed her eyes.

Her earliest memory was a faded one and confusing. She remembered the darkness of the hall as her Father carried her in and set her down on its tiled floor, which felt slippery under her feet. She remembered the wide curving staircase and its wooden handrail that beckoned her. Lisa's five-year-old immediate desire had been to slide down it, but as she dashed away from her father and raced up the stairs, a voice stopped her.

"Lisa! Ritorno! Come back here!" Her Mother's accent was still strong then and the sharp, clipped pronunciation of her upbringing was still evident. 'My Italian Countess' her father would say, enchanted by her rolling r's and lilting tone. Lisa remembered dragging her feet and hanging her head as she shuffled back to her Father, looking up and placing her little hand in his strong, warm one. He had winked, "Don't worry angel, you can explore later." And then he'd scooped her up and cradled her skinny legs on his forearm, holding her there as he marched through the hall towards the back of the building. She remembered feeling like they were walking into a black tunnel.

The move to the dark, cold manor house in a remote British countryside village had been a shock to the system for Lisa and her Mother Donnatella Danforth, an Italian Countess by birth who had met her father, Edward "Eddie" Danforth on a movie set in Portofino on the Italian Riviera. Eddie, a renowned Hollywood Director, had hired Donna's mansion for one of his films. It had been love, or at least passion, at first sight. They quickly became one of the hottest couples in LA and sealed their relationship with an ostentatious star-studded wedding in Malibu. Lisa had arrived less than nine months later, her birth a magazine feature feast of headlines from caustic to cute as she was presented as a testament to their passion. Up to this point, Donna and Lisa had spent their lives between the Italian estate and Eddie's multi million-dollar property in the hills above Hollywood, both of which were light, luxurious, warm and expansive places. And both paparazzi playgrounds. The latter had in part been the reason for Eddie's decision to uproot the family. He had bought the manor house in Hetherington nearly twenty years previously, an investment with the money from his early movie success, and by all accounts it had been a dilapidated mess. But for him it was a place he called home in his motherland. Whilst Donna and later Lisa, had spent all their time in warmer climbs, Eddie had travelled back and forth, overseeing the extensive reparations to the manor house and the brewery building that he had also purchased. Now, much of the restoration was complete and he wanted to return "home" and to a place that was away from the glare of the prying press. Lisa learnt later from her Mother, that she had tried with all her hot-blooded, Italian fiery dissent to prevent the move, but only one person was in control of this relationship and that was Eddie. Ultimately she had to accept; Eddie had declared he was moving there more or less permanently. If she wanted to be with him, she had no choice. So they did; though moving in the middle of November with the prospect of months of what seemed like endlessly grey skies might not have made for the best timing. Lisa's earliest memories were dominated by that greyness, that dark and damp pervasiveness of British winter that seemed to echo through the seemingly endless maze of rooms in the manor house. It was to have a profound impact on her inherently sunny soul.

Chapter 3

Doug stared at the pot of Extra Thick double cream as he took another slug of vodka from the bottle. He looked at his watch. Ten-thirty. He'd barely moved since Lisa had left an hour earlier but the bottle was now half empty and his mood was significantly darker. At first he'd been philosophical, he had to admit it might have been a bit tight of him to buy the pot on offer, but the more he thought about Lisa's reaction, the more humiliated he felt – and the angrier he became.

"Don't taste no different to Smirnoff to me," he said to no-one. "Russian innit? Well I'm British, and proud of it. Co-op vodka's good enough for me, so it should be good enough for anyone. S'pose you think you're above it cos you live in a manor house and got a Dame for a Mother. Or a Marchess, or whatever she is. Well you're a tart. And that makes you no better than me. We'll see about your hoity toity attitude."

Doug stared sullenly down at his big toe, sticking through a hole in his black socks. Somehow the fact he still had them on and there was a hole in them made him even angrier. He grabbed his jeans from where he had carelessly dropped them by the side of the bed and pulled them on, then swung his legs across and shoved his huge feet straight down into the hefty leather boots he wore out in the fields. Standing, he pulled his belt tight and buckled it like he meant business, then pulled his sweater over his head and grabbed his keys, marching towards the door. He hesitated as he put his hand on the knob and looked back at the bed. He strode back and picked up the pot of cream, "no point wastin' it. I'll give it to the wife, she'll make summat with it." He nodded at his positive attitude and grabbed the vodka at the same time. "And waste not want not." He glugged the last of its contents and threw the empty bottle back on the bed, "I'll teach you," he said, darkly, pointing at the bed as if Lisa was still on it.

Lisa's eyes snapped open. She blinked a little, confused as she recognized her surroundings. Her swing was still now, her head leaning on the chain, arms crossed in self comfort. She had completely lost track of time. She shook herself awake and looked at her watch. Close to eleven. She groaned and propelled herself from the seat, running across the park as fast as she could towards the manor. Despite the dark she hurtled down narrow lanes, brushing past overgrown bushes and over uneven ground with the speed and agility of both fitness and knowledge. Her feet knew this route by heart. As she approached the long drive she slowed, anxious not to tread too much on the telling-tales gravel that spread generously across its breadth. She knew she would be caught anyway, by the spying eye of another camera, but unless her Mother was in the monitor room, she would have some time to compose herself. She used the entry code and tip-toed through as the gates opened grandly before her. She walked carefully, sideways, to the soft verge, enjoying the sight of her footprints in the night time dew of the perfectly manicured grass. She could see a light glowing through one of the windows by the hall of the manor house as she approached. She sighed and swore to herself at her predicament. She hesitated for a moment and decided to take the kitchen entrance, praying silently that Peters would still be up, drinking a last cup of tea or making preparations for the following day. She ducked as she reached the building's grand façade, being careful not to cast a shadow from one of the tall Victorian street lamps that stood either side of the door. It meant creeping along the wall, a trick she was used to. Past the danger zone of being caught by her Mother if she was still awake, she scurried down the side of the house to the kitchen door. Gently, she turned the handle and let out a sigh of relief as she felt the latch give under the pressure of her hand. She opened it cautiously, no more than a couple of inches, then peered in. Instantly she felt a familiar flood of love and safety as she saw Peters, who turned round to look at her. She pushed the door open wider and crept across the stone tiled floor. Peters, standing in her striped cotton pyjamas, gave her a wry look and put her finger to her mouth, indicating she should stay quiet. Lisa snuggled up to her and Peters put a protective arm around her. Lisa whispered in her ear,

"Is she still up?"

Peters looked regretfully at her, "she's still up and she's waiting for you. You're not going to get out of it my Angel. Let's just see if we can make it as painless as possible." Peters winked at Lisa and held her tighter. But it did little to appease her.

"Is she angry?" Lisa's whisper was more urgent.

"Well. She's agitated, let's put it that way. I'm sorry love, you know what she's like when you don't obey the rules."

Lisa nodded forlornly. Peters gently let go and spun her round to hold her shoulders. "Let's do it together ok? I'll serve her tea and you come with me. Try to be light, alright?" Lisa nodded. Peters squeezed her hand, picked up the tea tray and headed determinedly for the door.

Donna was sitting in the small study that lead off from the front of the entrance hall. A reading lamp glowed on the wide mahogany desk, the light Lisa had seen from the driveway. She was leaning back in the deep leather chair her Father had once occupied when he worked. Her glasses were perched on her nose as she read a book spread out in her lap. Lisa took a deep breath as they approached.

"Tea!" announced Peters as she placed the silver tray on the end of the imposing desk.

"So I see," replied Donna without looking up. "Pour. Please." Her tone was clipped. Lisa shrank inwardly. The signs were not good. Her Mother had not acknowledged her.

"Hello Mother," her voice came out like a squeak as the saliva dried from her mouth.

"Lisa." She still hadn't looked up. Lisa shot a glance at Peters, who was pouring very slowly from the China teapot. She took a little comfort from her presence and her surreptitious wink.

"Could you be any slower Peters?" asked Donna sarcastically.

"Possibly. But then I fear the tea would be beyond 'temperatura perfetta'."

"Don't be sarcastic Peters."

Peters allowed her eyebrow to rise in irony.

"… and your presence will make no difference'" Donna flicked her immaculately manicured hand at Peters, still without looking up. And then she addressed her daughter.

"Where have you been?"

Lisa felt her heart move up into her throat until it felt like she wouldn't be able to force any words past it. She told herself to be calm.

"With Doug." Her voice was tiny.

"You left him nearly two hours ago. He's just left."

Lisa gulped and the sound echoed loudly in her ears. "He came here?"

Donna finally raised her head and looked her daughter straight in the eyes. "Yes."

The word hung in the air and the only sound now came from the domed carriage clock that sat on the bookshelf behind Donna. It sounded like a ticking time bomb. Lisa felt compelled to break the silence, as always.

"Why?"

Donna sighed and removed her glasses. She leant her head to one side resting her chin on her hand, regarded her daughter thoughtfully. Her voice softened.

"Darling, you can't just pick and choose. You can't just say no."

The hairs on Lisa's neck prickled at the gentleness of her tone.

"Where were you?" Donna became nonchalant again as she replaced her glasses and returned her attention to her book.

"In the park."

"You know I'll know don't you?"

"Yes Mother. I was in the park. On the swings. I lost track of time."

The controlling, unbearably loaded silence fell again. And again Lisa responded to its invitation.

"Honestly, that's where I was. And you will see it."

"The swings," Donna was disdainful, "don't you think you're getting a little bit too old for the swings, darling?"

Lisa threw a glance at Peters, she could tell where this was leading, she needed help. Peters picked up the tray.

"Should I take Lisa for a cocoa perhaps?"

"Shut up, Peters, I haven't finished as you well know."

Peters looked rueful, but complied. She knew when to pick her moments with Donna.

"I asked you a question darling."

"I'll never be too old for them." Lisa suddenly felt the anger rise and became petulant. Peters closed her eyes. The pattern was in full flow. There was nothing she could do now.

"Well, that's rather a shame isn't it? Because my daughter needs to learn to grow up. She needs to remember the rules. And she needs to understand that when she has work to do, she can't just say no."

Donna snapped the book shut and looked at Lisa again.

"Doesn't she?"

Lisa felt the bile rise in her throat and was about to object when she felt Peters stare boring into her.

"Yes Mother."

"And what is the most important thing we have to remember about the freedom and joy we have in our village?"

"Sharing is caring." Lisa delivered the expected mantra.

"Indeed."

And then the bombshell dropped.

"So we are agreed then, that you need some quiet time don't you?"

Lisa's face crumpled and she let out the familiar plea that she knew would deliver absolutely no positive result at all.

"Noooo, please… Mother…."

"Enough!" Donna raised her hand, taking the opportunity to inspect her fingernails as she did so, "Peters, take Lisa to the Quiet Room please. She needs to understand…"

"But Mother please…"

"No, Lisa. If you want to keep out of the Quiet Room, you must learn to abide by the rules. It's really very simple." Donna breathed in deeply, closed her eyes and then exhaled in a long slow stream of air, "it's always been so very simple." She took in another full breath and her gentle tone resumed, "that's settled. Peters? Just until dawn. After all, tomorrow is a special day and we don't want it spoiled by any silly behaviour, do we?"

Peters gave Lisa a resigned look and placed a hand on her back, a gentle hint that she needed to leave it there. Lisa shut her eyes and swallowed the words she wanted say, feeling them burn as they slid back down her throat. She opened her eyes again and took Peters hand compliantly.

Peters smiled, "good girl." They headed towards the door as Donna threw a last comment.

"And Peters. Before you go to bed, bring me my yoga mat. I'm feeling rather stressed."

Peters flicked a sideways glance at Lisa, raising a sardonic eyebrow, "yes, of course."

They continued through the door and Peters closed it quietly behind them, the click of its latch in sync with the start of Lisa's falling tears. Peters held her briefly as she sobbed. "It's only until dawn. Come on. Let's get it over with."

Lisa wiped at the salty stream falling on her cheeks and dragged her feet along the hallway. Peters couldn't help but laugh.

"It's not funny!" Lisa mumbled miserably.

"I know, but you're just like you were as a child, dragging your feet like that. I can't help it. Makes me see you at ten years old wearing grubby dungarees and carrying a bucket of worms." Peters giggled. It had the desired affect. Lisa, though trying hard not to, couldn't help but smile.

"They weren't worms. They were maggots." Lisa protested.

"Oh of course, maggots, much more sensible than worms." Peters laughed again. "I remember the time you dropped them near your Mother's feet. I've never seen her move so fast."

Lisa giggled, "served her right. Wish I had some now." She became serious again. "Peters, I'm going to be Twenty-eight tomorrow. Twenty-eight! And I'm still trapped in this prison."

"But you know she will treat you like a Princess tomorrow. The World will be yours."

"I don't want to be treated like a Princess for one day of the year! I just want to be normal all the rest of the days."

Peters opened the creaky door that lead to the vast network of cellar rooms and flicked a light switch to illuminate the the cold stone steps that wound down into the dark corridors.

"And what's normal?" she threw back at Lisa with a heavy tone of irony.

Lisa huffed, "fucked if I know. You tell me. I've spent all my life here… being forced to believe this is normal. But I know that it's not."

"No." It was all that Peters could say as they approached a huge white padded door. Lisa took a deep breath.

"Ok."

Peters pushed the door open and Lisa walked through, her eyes shut and hands firmly over them. Peters blinked at the stark light in the astoundingly bright room. The glare from the naked bulb bounced around the completely white walls, floor and ceiling, making her eyeballs smart with pain as they adjusted to its flashing harshness. She guided Lisa to the bed with its white sheets, white frame, white hand restraints.

"Now, we're not going to need these are we?"

Lisa peeped through a slit in her fingers and Peters pointed at the restraints. Lisa shook her head.

"Good girl. Settle yourself down. It's only a few hours, stay calm and I'll be here right on time, ok?"

Lisa nodded as she lay on the cold sheets and turned on her side, drawing her knees up to to a foetal position.

Peter's stoked her hair gently and mouthed "I'm so sorry" silently, as she briefly held Lisa's hand. Then she turned and left the room, the light still glaring. As she closed the door, her demeanour changed.

"Bitch!" She clenched her fists, arms stiff with anger, "whatever has been done to you, there's no justification for this," she spat the words as she passed along the corridor, smacking the wall and letting out an anguished cry, just as she always did. By the time she reached the top of the basement stairs, she was calm again and ready to face Donna. She sidetracked into the gym and grabbed a yoga mat and then marched back to the small office, where Donna has moved to the monitoring booth and was watching a screen intently. She didn't look up as Peters entered the room.

"No restraints?" she said it casually.

"Not necessary," Peters equaled her tone.

"We'll see." Donna turned and held her hand out for the mat, which Peters placed with an accidental slap into her hand.

Donna did not flinch.

"That will be all for tonight Peters. Are we prepared for tomorrow?"

"Yes. Goodnight." Peters did not care to elaborate on the birthday plans for Lisa's special day. She was fully aware it was more about Donna than her daughter. She span on her heel and Donna watched her walk out, an amused smile playing on her mouth. Turning her attention back to the screen, she sighed happily as she watched her daughter sleeping.

"We're going to have such a wonderful day tomorrow my darling," She stroked the screen. It gave her the surrogate feeling of comforting her daughter, an act she rarely performed with her personally, "I love birthdays."

Chapter 4

Doug sat at the tiny breakfast bar in the cosy kitchen of the little cottage that was home for him and his wife Angela and their big black Alsatian, Dante. He looked down into his pot of Extra Thick cream as he twiddled it round and round. Angela, leaning against the cooker, arms folded, was tired after her lunchtime session in the Fish & Chip van. They'd run out of haddock and she'd taken a good portion of abuse from unhappy customers. Even free fish fingers hadn't appeased her regulars and she'd had a bellyful. She really didn't need to deal with one of Doug's moods. But she knew any form of conflict or disagreement with his grumpiness would just make things worse. She leaned over and took the pot from him and examined the label, "well it's dated yesterday, so it shouldn't be off!" She looked at Doug quizzically. He shrugged his shoulders.

"Maybe the fridge ain't working properly."

"There's nothing wrong with our fridge. More likely the fridge in the shop."

She gingerly put her nose near the pot and took the smallest of sniffs. "Oh fuck. Yes, that's off." She stamped hard on the foot pedal of the bin by her side, angry with the pot for making her feel nauseous. The bin lid flew open at a speed that tested its hinges and she dropped what was left of the cream in it. Doug threw his hands up in the air in exasperation.

"I wanted crumble! Can't you even make me a crumble with it? Least get something out of it?"

"Darling I'll make you a crumble and some custard. Nice and thick and creamy." She leaned over and ruffled his thick head of hair and tried to kiss him.

"Get off, you smell of cod." He shrugged her away.

Angela ignored his comment and returned to their conversation about his distress over the afternoon's events, "so she refused because it was off? Completely?"

"Yes," he said miserably, "and cos my vodka wasn't Smirnoff."

She ruffled his hair again, "doesn't seem very reasonable, must have been something else. Was there?"

"Nope, she just jumped off the bed and disappeared. And she scored my card. Bloody bitch."

Doug's annoyance was rising once more. Angela tried to calm him,

"Come on, don't get angry. We'll deal with all that with Theresa. And we'll just have to make up for it, won't we?" she said, slapping her muscular buttock.

"Not while you smell of cod."

"The Fish & Chip Van is easy money Doug. It might be a bit of a bugger getting the deep fried smell out, but it's worth it," she said reasonably, "so why don't you get a beer, I'll have a shower, then I'll get going on that crumble. Alright?"

"S'pose." Doug rose and opened the fridge, scanning the shelves for a lager, "and don't forget the custard."

Angela smiled, she still knew how to perk her man up, "I'll make you the best custard you ever had."

Chapter 5

Lisa counted mentally, passing the seconds and minutes "...fifty-five Mississippi, fifty-six Mississippi, fifty-seven Mississippi, fifty-eight Mississippi, fifty-nine Mississippi, nine minutes, one Mississippi..." It was a strategy she had developed over the years to keep some idea of time and to help didtract her mind from the destructive, oppressive thoughts that would otherwise have filled it in the bleak silence of the White Room. Sometimes if she was lucky it lulled her to sleep quite quickly as it became like a rolling mental hum. But not tonight. In the last few weeks, with Peters help she'd finally started to break free of the grip her Mother and the village had on her. Tonight her thoughts were full of the questions that came from a newly acquired clarity in her head. It was like a fog had lifted, as if she had emerged from the automaton like feeling of her life and emerged into a new light. The problem was what that light revealed; that she had a mass of questions and very few answers. The frustration of that was adding to the anger that she could feel rising over the wasted years. The unutterably sad feeling that she would be twenty-eight years old the next day and yet she felt as if her adult life had not even started. Well, that her own life had not started. The one she had been living up until now, was the life her Mother wanted for her. Shaped and controlled for her by Donna. She had already determined that the next year would be pivotal, that she would change everything, though in this moment she did not have an idea about what that change would look like, it had to be better than the miserable existence she had now. As she floated in the familiar white sea of despair in the Quiet Room, tonight she finally felt that she might actually be able to swim. In what direction was not clear, but at least she could feel like there was hope if she just started moving through the water. Perhaps she should start by swimming back to the past.

Whilst the darkness and grey damp of the hall and her new home had at first felt somehow alien, in that typical innocent child's way of finding the happiness in life, she had reveled in the exploration of rooms and corridors of what she thought of as her castle. And she delighted in the gardens and meadows that spread out from the manor walls, like a vast children's playground, with plants to touch and smell, creatures to make friends with - and so much mud! And unlike the restrictive, contained and manicured life in the sunny place she came from, here she found far more freedom. Partly because her father encouraged it and partly because her Mother was constantly something called 'stanco di chio' – tired of it! Lisa would come flying into the hall with some 'disgusting creature' in her hand and show it excitedly to her Father, who would bend down and ask her "What have you found today my Angel?", whilst her Mother would invariably throw her expressive arms up into the air and flounce away down the hallway talking loudly to herself in Italian. Lisa was vaguely aware that her behavior was a delight for one parent and a disappointment to the other, but if there had to be a choice, then the active enjoyment of muddy fun in the garden was going to win every time over a quiet afternoon with a book whilst her Mother read the imported Italian and American glossy magazines that she loved, occasionally updating her oblivious daughter about the social lives of friends.

As she thought back, she recalled a conversation between her Mother and her Father on the subject. Her recall had been stimulated by Peters earlier comment about the worms. She would have been about ten years old. Lisa remembered being out in the garden, she had her bucket and spade and a little fishing net in a miniature wooden wheelbarrow her Father had asked the manor's handyman, Alfred, to make for her. She had trundled down towards the pond, pushing the barrow with intent, determined in her goal to catch some tadpoles. As she passed by the compost pile, she'd spotted a rubbish bag that had split, it's content spewing out across the lawn – alive with what her awe struck mind had thought must have been a million little creamy worms. Thrilled, she'd taken her bucket and spade from the barrow and rushed over to scoop some up. Almost giddy with excitement she remembered being fascinated by their squirming mass of activity in the bottom of the pail. She must show them to her Father! She abandoned the wheelbarrow and ran as fast as her legs would take her back to the hall. As she flew in through the kitchen door, she almost knocked a startled Peters of her feet.

"Hey slow down, where's the fire?"

"Creamy worms for Daddy! Look!" She'd held the bucket out for Peters, who for some reason seemed less than excited by what she saw. Undeterred, Lisa ran towards the hall.

"Daddy? Daddy?" she poked her head into open doors on either side of the hallway in search of her Father. Becoming a little frustrated, her shouts became louder, until he emerged, from a small living room he used for reading. As she lay now and recalled the scenes, she couldn't quite work out whether she had recognized at the time that he was disheveled and hot and flustered, or whether that was something she was only just recognizing, but whichever, it now became recognizable to her that it was a pivotal moment in her relationship with him. He had closed the door behind him and rushed over to her, somewhat over zealous in his enthusiasm

"Angel! What have you got there?"

Excitedly she held the bucket up to him just as her Mother made her way languorously down the stairs to see what all the commotion was about.

"Creamy worms Daddy, look!"

Her Father had burst out laughing and opened his arms wide to pull her in for a hug. The sequence of events from there was a little confused to her now, but three things had happened. As he picked her up, she had lost her grip on the bucket and it fell to the floor, spilling the squirming mass of maggots across the parquet. She had found herself in his embrace – and looking over his shoulder saw a woman come out of the living room he had been in. Also rather disheveled and moving quickly along the wall towards the kitchen at the back of the manor. Lisa recognized her as someone who came in to work. And then there was Donna, who had arrived at the base of the stairs just in time to see the maggots engulf her shoes. She shrieked.

"Oh My God. What is this disgusting mess? What have you done to my Mui Muis? You revolting child!"

Shrieking again, she had stepped out of her diamante studded high heels and flicked her hands frantically at the maggots that were clinging to her sheer-stockinged feet. "Cazzo vai via! Aiii fungula! Creature disgustose! Merde!!

Hopping from one foot to another and leaving a mess of

crushed maggots in her wake, she looked for all the World to Lisa like a mad person - and as her Father started to bellow with laughter, Lisa followed suit.

"Figlio di puttana! What did I do to deserve a child like you?" Donna was furious, humiliated. "Look at you. You don't even look like me. Blond, like your Father, as if he were your only parent. And like a little boy, a muddy, clumsy, little urchin."

"Donna!" Her Father stopped laughing and roared at her Mother. Lisa nestled into his neck, at the time not terribly aware of the meaning of her Mother's words, but knowing they were hurtful and that she had done something terribly wrong. And her Father's roar was frightening.

Donna slammed each of her shoes against the staircase, desperate to rid them of the wriggling invaders.

"And do you think you could be a little more discreet with your tart?"

Her Father did not respond, but released her onto the floor and cupped her cheeks with his safe, warms hands and looked right into her eyes. "You're beautiful my Angel, you hear? Your Mother is upset, but it's not your fault. Ok?"

She nodded. Still not understanding what was happening. He took her hand.

"Come on, we'll have this mess cleaned up and we'll go and get some milk and biscuits."

She followed him as he headed for the kitchen, tripping as she tried to keep up with his big strides. He completely ignored her now sobbing Mother, who was trying to hook out a maggot that had taken refuge between her toes.

"Sorry Mummy," she had said sheepishly as she had passed her. But her Mother had not acknowledged her apology.

Hurrying along by her Father, feeling now rather worried, she was glad to feel the warmth of the kitchen. When they got there, the woman who had come out of the living room was hurriedly tying her hair up in a bun. "Conchita we'd like some milk and cookies, wouldn't we Angel?" He had turned to her and softly pinched her cheek, "don't be worried little one, everything's ok. Conchita is one of Daddy's most special friends and she's going to get us something delicious, right

Conchita?" He had looked up at her for her response, "Si, milch in cookers, yayss…" the woman had spun around the kitchen opening cupboard doors and drawers, clearly unfamiliar with their contents, but anxiously determined to find what she needed and do as her Father had asked. Meanwhile her Father had propped her up on a bar stool and sat stroking her hair, but though she liked the reassuring touch of his hand, she suddenly felt bewildered and overcome and the tears started flowing.

He pulled a handkerchief from his pocket and dabbed at her eyes, then scooped her into his arms again as Conchita placed the milk and cookies onto the breakfast bar for them.

"Say thank you to Conchita, Lisa."

She obeyed, but inside she wished she would go away. She sounded strange and she smelt funny too.

Her Father cradled her chin in his hand and lifted her face to look into his eyes. "Mummy didn't mean what she said. She's upset about lots of things and she got angry because she felt silly. Ok?"

"Ok," sobbed Lisa, but she really didn't feel ok.

"Good girl. Now. Stop the crying and let's eat our cookies."

As Lisa lay in the White Room now and looked back at that little girl, she recognized a moment in her life that had been buried deep in her subconscious. It spurred the thought that when you are that young, it was amazing how a single sentence could break you, even though you did not recognize it at the time. Now, that sentence echoed in her mind as she finally drifted into sleep, "what did I do to deserve a child like you…"

Chapter 6

The small village Post Office was busy when Doug and Angela arrived to discuss the Extra Thick Cream incident with the postmistress, Theresa, who happened also to be the most influential and formidable person in the community. Well second most influential. The first was actually The Lady of the Manor herself and Doug had already pressed that button. The two of them strode in and headed straight for the tiny counter at the back of the building, bypassing Theresa's husband Roy, who, after much discussion, they had decided was really the one to blame for the whole situation. It was, after all, his cream that had been off. As they walked single file through the canned goods and personal hygiene items, they glanced at each other for reassurance. Doug reached the counter first. Theresa, head down, was busy with paperwork. Doug coughed for attention and she immediately held a warning finger up as she added up a row of figures. Doug fell silent and waited patiently. Theresa scribbled a number and looked up. She offered a flat smile.

"Yes?"

Doug sucked air into his chest and stood tall.

"I'm here to talk to you about your husband's cream."

Theresa stared at him not a flicker of a response on her face. Doug shuffled his feet uncomfortably, waiting for permission to speak further. Angela prodded him in the back.

"Er. It was off," blurted out Doug, "swatting at his wife's hand to let her know he had this.

"What? When? How? I'm going to need a bit more than that," she responded irritatedly.

"Yes. Of course. Well, see, I bought a pot of Extra Thick cream on Monday. 'Twas on offer cos it was on its Sell By Date. I put it in the fridge. On Tuesday I took it out of the fridge and it was off. Already. Which really it shouldn't of been."

Theresa stared at him. "See Roy," she said dismissively and went back to her figures.

"No."

She looked up sharply, unaccustomed to dissention. Angela poked Doug in the back again and once again her swatted her away, but harder this time.

"Well it's more complicated than just the cream."

Theresa sighed.

"Well maybe you should tell me how it can be more complicated than your cream being off. Quickly."

"Well. I bought it for one of my sessions with Lisa and 'cos it was off, she refused AND…" at this point Doug raised his index finger to indicate he was getting to the crux of the matter, "she marked off my session even though I didn't get nothing."

Theresa regarded him eye to eye for a moment.

"So she refused completely on the basis that the cream was off?"

"Yes."

"There weren't any other circumstances. No provocation, distress of any other kind?"

Theresa eyed him suspiciously. Doug's manliness often got the better of him. He wasn't averse to dishing out a helping of sexism. She wanted to be sure he hadn't needled Lisa. It wouldn't be the first time. He held her stare.

"No."

Angela dug him in the back again.

"Well no, apart from she didn't like that I didn't have Smirnoff."

"What?" Theresa frowned, confused.

Doug turned to Angela and hissed, "I told you that would just confuse it." He turned back to Theresa. "I wanted to use Vodka as well, but I didn't have Smirnoff. Just Co-op."

Theresa put her head in her hand. Sometimes she needed strength not to respond to some of the abject pettiness that surrounded her. The moment's hesitance prevented her from admonishing him. Ultimately it would not affect his sense of grievance, it wasn't worth the aggravation to argue. She looked up again.

"Alright. We'll reinstate the session. Not because of the cream, you understand. It could just as well have been a problem with your fridge."

"But I…"

Angela poked him in the back again. Once too often. He spun round.

"Will you keep your fucking finger to yourself woman! I don't need it!" He turned back to Theresa.

"Actually Angela is right. There are no buts," she said, pulling herself up to her full height of authority. "You'll get your session back because the principal of refusing you is not acceptable. As for the cream, unless you bring the pot back in, we can't judge it. So you'll just have to swallow that one."

Doug nodded. "Fair enough. I'll take that."

Theresa clicked her fingers at him.

"What?"

"Your card. Hand it over."

Doug took the card from his back pocket and watched her carefully as she added a credit to his account. Now he was satisfied. Well almost.

"Good. Sorted." He took the card back. "I think you need to have a word with Lisa," he ventured. Angela sucked her breath in.

"That will be for me to decide Doug. You're done. I'll see you on Sunday."

Doug hesitated, momentarily reluctant to let go of the chance to pursue Lisa's punishment. After all, she had humiliated him. But taking Theresa on took balls - and he knew if he got on the wrong side of her, his own fate would be a darn sight worse than Lisa's. Her voice had that edge of danger in it, a warning he might be about to cross the line. He concluded it wasn't worth the risk and relented. Nodding his acceptance of her final word on the matter, he turned on his heel, indicating at his wife that she should do the same, then they both made their way back through the store. Theresa watched them leave and as the door closed behind them, she glanced over at Roy, who was carefully rearranging his nuts. She tapped her lip, momentarily distracted by the thought that he was wasting his time with his new 'Health' section. It was squeezed in between the pickles and the canned vegetables, comprised of nuts and dried fruits plus a few vitamins.

"Just had a complaint from Doug about your cream."

Roy sighed as he looked at a packet of shriveled raisins. He knew how they felt. "And?"

"Maybe you should be a bit more careful about your Sell-By Offers."

24

He nodded and Theresa continued.

"I think there's something going on with Lisa. She's being very rebellious."

Roy shrugged and wondered if his apricots and prunes would make a good window display.

"I'll deal with it." Theresa announced what Roy already knew would be the upshot of the conversation. There was rarely a need to actively participate in a debate with his wife, she always drew her own conclusion regardless of his contribution. His silence generally saved a pointless argument he would inevitably lose.

"She's a good one that Lisa." He added after the fact. Theresa stared at him.

"That's as may be. But The Club comes first."

Chapter 7

Lisa's eyes snapped open as she felt Peters gently stroking her arm.

"Good morning Angel."

"Hey." Lisa rubbed her eyes and stretched.

"I know this isn't the ideal place to feel like today is a celebration, but Happy Birthday my sweet."

Lisa smiled up at the woman she regarded as her guardian, her protector, her comfort. "Thank you. Really. For everything. I don't know what I would do without you." Peters smiled and pinched her cheek, just like her Father used to.

"You're a ray of sunshine." She handed Lisa a glass of orange juice and watched as she gulped it down, smiling at the way her almost clear eyebrows lifted in the simple joy of some fluid to quench her thirst and the way her eyes sparkled despite everything she had to endure. She felt a sudden pang of anguish in her heart at this beautiful woman's innocent, sunny demeanour in spite of the way she had been forced to live her life. For the most part, Peters tried to keep these kind of thoughts at bay, but Lisa's recent determination to break the grip of her Mother and the secrets of the village meant she would have to face the consequences of her collusion. It was not going to be an easy thing to see it through but it would certainly be the right thing. For Peters, whose arrival at the Manor had almost been followed by her immediate departure, the tender little life that was Lisa, had been the only reason for staying. She had somehow known that she would eventually have the opportunity to help set the girl free. It had sometimes been excruciatingly difficult not to break apart the girl's ignorance of the fact she was not living a life within the typical framework of social boundaries. Often it was Lisa's lack of understanding of the fact her life was not "normal" that protected her sanity. Peters was acutely aware that the girl's recovery from the emotional impact of coming to terms with a plight she hadn't previously understood herself to be in, was going to take some time and support. And therapy. She was grateful that it was Lisa herself who had started the process of breaking the chains. But that would be in the future. For today, they still had to play the game. Peters looked at her watch.

"It's just past five. Let's get you back to your room and you can relax, have a shower and get yourself dressed ready for breakfast. Ok?"

Lisa nodded, downing the last little bit of juice and handing the glass back to Peters.

"Yes." She said it with determination. She gave Peters a bright smile. "It's all good. You know what? I feel stronger and more powerful and more 'me' than I have since… well since I was a kid…." she paused, "you know what I mean, when I say 'me'?"

"I do. And it's a pleasure for me to see. You're my shiny birthday Angel today. I'm proud of you."

Lisa squeezed Peters hand as she passed her and headed for the door, "you know what? Today is my day. And I'm going to own it."

Now, exactly ten years on, as she stood in her bathroom and stared at herself in the mirror, the memories kept on coming, like she had a need to completely revisit the past in order to let it go.

Soon after the incident with the creamy worms, Conchita had left the staff of the manor house. To be replaced by Frederica. And then Sienna, Tamsin, Greta, Philomena, Delores…. and a stream of others. In fact, there was very little stability in the staff, only Alfred and Peters were there throughout, the rest came and went in a whirlwind of constant change. Sometimes they would leave after they caused arguments between Mummy and Daddy because they had stepped out of line or upset Donna in some way that Lisa never really understood, but more often they just disappeared with no explanation, their names never to be mentioned again.

Lisa had carried on with her childhood fun as far as she could. She was schooled at home and her tutors would be there between nine in the morning and four in the afternoon on weekdays, which left the rest of those days and the weekend for playing. When her Father was there, she could spend much of her spare time in the garden, run wild around the rooms and secret places of the house and indulge in the sports she loved. Like tennis and fishing, cricket on the lawn and the occasional game of football. But this was interspersed with periods of complete shut down when her Father left to film on location. Times

27

she dreaded. When she would be in the tight grip of control that her Mother exerted. Life became rigid and full of rules and she would have to wear dresses, have ribbons in her hair, sit quietly in the drawing room and other forms of imprisonment of her spirit that she hated. During these periods, the time dragged and her brain felt it might burst with frustration and boredom – and when her temper would be tested to its maximum. In these periods, she relied on the support and comfort she received from Peters and Alfred. She regarded Alfred like the Uncle she didn't have. He was rough, burly and gruff, but also kind and gentle and he taught her how to use the fascinating tools he kept in his shed. And Peters she simply loved and adored. There was a piece of her that had wished Peters were her Mummy, though it was a difficult thought because it also made her feel ashamed and ungrateful that she could not feel that way about her own Mother. But Peters protected her and encouraged her to be free and enjoy the things she loved in a way that Donna did not seem to be able. And Lisa was fully aware that without Peters as an ally, her life would be considerably worse. Donna's capacity for punishment was endless and inventive. And as the years passed, Lisa seemed to fall foul of her on a more and more frequent basis. Somehow she just could not do anything right for her Mother.

She first experienced the White Room when she was twelve. The space had originally been created to film a scene for one of her Father's movies and after that had finished it had stayed locked; one of the few places she was not allowed to enter. Until, that was, the day she 'pushed her Mother too far.' It was spring time, when emerging from the long dark days of winter meant that the energy she had stored up could be released with a burst of joy. It became one of her favourite times of year. On this particular 'first really sunny day', when all British people seem go a bit mad after the confinement of the grey season, Lisa had made a plan to test drive a go-kart around the extensive lawns. She had been gradually building her super vehicle through the winter, secretly, in one of Alfred's garden sheds. She'd gathered the various components she needed, with his help and he'd leant her his tools for construction. She was delighted with the result. The bolted cross plank that was the front suspension moved beautifully when she pulled on the steering strings she'd attached to them near the wheels. She'd found an old box in the cellar that she had nailed to the rear suspension to form the seat. She'd even painted it with the racing colours of the cars she'd seen in The Italian Job. It was, even though she said so herself, a thing of magnificence. She couldn't wait to try it out. So when that first really sunny day arrived, at four o'clock, straight after her maths lesson, she had raced to the shed to bring out her pride and joy. Then she'd pulled it all the way to the top of the track that led from the garden sheds down to the pond at the edge of the estate. She sat on it, looking with glee at the pathway before her, thinking how fun it was that she was going to able to get great momentum up and fly down there on her amazing new vehicle. She positioned herself just right, with her feet on the front suspension, took up the rope and rocked herself gently until the kart began to move. Giggling gleefully, she felt a huge thrill as it started to generate speed, slowly at first and then quicker. She tugged gently with the strings to steer and found herself feeling a sense of flying. Wow!!! Wheeeeeeee…. she had never felt such exhilaration! She leaned forward into the speed, seeking to generate even more of a thrill. Until, that was, at a speed that was becoming slightly greater than she felt she could handle, the sudden realization hit her, that she had no brakes – and therefore no way of stopping. Now her adrenaline stopped feeding excitement and diverted its energy to panic. She tried to pull back on the strings, but that just de-stabilised the front of the kart and made her feel like she might flip it and fly off it backwards. So she held on as it careered over the gravel, her heart thumping in her throat so hard she thought it might burst out. Now her brain was focused on how to crash land without too much damage. Her chosen destination was the pond. It was a relatively short distance between the path and the expanse of water, over an area of fairly flat grass. She needed to steer a little to the left and she thought she could make it. That was her only way of thinking she might have a soft landing. As she reached her chosen exit point, she held her breath and tugged on the left string, feeling the bumping, careering progress crash through every bone in her body as the kart hurtled over the grass and left the ground briefly at the edge of the pond, landing with a resounding smack on the water. She felt the silence and the cold as she catapulted off it and plunged into the reedy, dark green water. She watched the slow motion decent of the kart a couple of feet away. It seemed at first that it might float and for a few moments after its initial dunking, it headed for the surface. But then the weight of the metal wheels and the box seat got the better of it and pulled it back into the murky depths. For a moment she felt an eerie sense of peace amongst the swaying reed, until she suddenly become aware of her own sinking feeling. She started to pull her arms against the water, eyes focused on the dull light above that was trying hard to penetrate the darkness around her. She paddled her legs, freeing them from the reeds that had enveloped her in a kind of soft embrace and started to feel her body move slowly up through the gloom. She broke through the surface just as her lungs started to burn, gulping a huge breath of air a little too quickly, making her choke and splutter on the disgusting green fluid that filled her mouth. She felt relief rush through her as she spat out the gobby water and then flipped on her back, floating on the surface and looking up at the blue sky, thanking her lucky stars for a narrow escape. But relief did not last long. She heard the familiar shriek of her Mother's voice as she urged Alfred to run faster towards the pond and then the noisy splashing as he rushed and grabbed her collar, dragging her unceremoniously up onto the grass and dumping her like a wet fish onto the ground. She winced as her bum thudded onto a mole's mound and then felt the air rush from her lungs as the impact of her back on the hard earth winded her. A little stunned, she looked up into the concerned eyes of Alfred, her Mother looming over his shoulder, screeching at him.

"Is she alright? Oh my God, is she alive?"

She felt Alfred press his fingers into her wrist, the pressure hurting her skin,

"Yes ma'am, she's alive." He pronounced.

Lisa got her breath back and struggled to sit up, making it quite clear that she was not only alive, but absolutely fine. Which was a mistake. She should have stayed where she was and feigned injury of some sort, it might have saved the wrath that now whipped her.

"You little bastard! You little bastard!" her Mother screamed at her, clenching her fists in fury, "how dare you frighten me like that! What is wrong with you? I thought you'd killed yourself. You little bastard!"

Lisa's twelve-year-old brain couldn't work out how such anger related to the fact she was ok.

"Sorry Mummy," she said, in the tiniest of voices.

Her Mother stood with one hand on her hip, the other holding her forehead. Her face, which rarely showed colour because of her olive complexion, was a sort of dirty grey. Alfred, seeing what was about to happen, managed to get across to her just in time to catch her in his arms as she fainted, propping her limp body up against his chest.

Lisa began to wail. "Oh noooooo, Mummy," she ran over to where Alfred was, "have I killed Mummy?" she asked desperately.

"Lord no child, she's just fainted, everything's alright. Just you follow me, we'll take her back to the house and she'll be right as rain after a rest."

Alfred scooped up the dead weight of Donna's limp body easily in his strong arms and strode up and over the bank towards the house. Lisa trailed miserably along behind, still sobbing.

An hour later, she had been stripped of her clothing, placed in a hot bath, scrubbed and re-emerged to be dressed in a soft blue floral pinafore and matching patent shoes. Then she was told to wait in her room for her Mother. She sat on the end of her bed and swung her feet, feeling uncomfortable and miserable. She had her favourite teddy under her arm for comfort. When Donna finally entered the room, Lisa felt a sense of foreboding. She hung her head, too frightened to look up. Donna paced backwards and forwards. Minutes passed. Lisa could feel her Mother's eyes on her in the heaviness of the atmosphere, the silence broken only by the soft swish of her mules on the deep pile carpet. Then the movement stopped. Lisa glanced up momentarily. Donna was staring out of the window towards the pond.

"I don't understand you," she said finally.

Lisa didn't know how to respond.

"And I don't know what to do with you. I despair at your rebelliousness," she was shaking her head, "at your utter lack of decorum, your complete disregard for anything feminine. Sometimes I think you should have been a boy." Donna turned round to look at her daughter. "If your hair were to be cut short right now, I swear you would be mistaken for a boy in your stupid dungarees and plimsoles. Always playing boys games and fiddling with nuts and bolts and… and… bits of wood! I don't know, what it is you do out there in that garden each day. Coming in dirty and stinking, like you were being brought up in a workman's cottage instead of this beautiful manor house."

31

Lisa sat quietly, figuring quite correctly that any response would be the wrong one at this point.

"And when I try to teach you, when I give you the benefit of my help or advice, you reject it. As if there is nothing that I have that you might want or could possibly learn from. It's all about your Father. Everything. I may as well not be your Mother."

Lisa was confused.

"I love you Mummy." It was all she could think of to say.

"Oh please. Don't use that word. It's an insult to my intelligence."

Lisa frowned, why was it a bad thing to say she loved her Mummy? The silence settled again until Donna let out a deep sigh and turned to her. Now her voice was gentle.

"You need to learn a lesson. You need to understand that you must change your ways. I've prepared some Quiet Time for you somewhere where you can think about what you have done."

Her Mother's soft tone and the prospect of being left to herself soothed her. To Lisa at this point, what her Mother was proposing sounded quite attractive. If it meant she didn't have to sit in the drawing room and be elegant and that she could play away from her, then it had to be an improvement on her current circumstances. It would not be long before she would realise how very wrong she was.

Donna turned on her heels, still without looking at Lisa and as she passed by her where she sat on her bed, she clicked her fingers. Lisa instantly sprang to her feet.

"Follow me." Donna said sharply, "and leave that toy on your bed."

Lisa obediently dropped Teddy Eddie and traipsed behind her Mother in silence as they descended the grand stairway and into the hall. They marched towards the basement door and at this point, Lisa started to feel uncomfortable.

"May I have cookies with Peters first please? I'm very hungry," she asked in a quiet pleading voice, looking up into her Mother's dark eyes.

"Peters is away today. She's visiting a sick relative. You are on your own."

Lisa felt herself starting to tremble. She was frightened.

"Alfred will bring you some milk and cookies when we have settled you in." Donna opened the cellar door and ushered Lisa through as she switched on the light.

"Where are we going Mummy?"

"You'll see."

They went down the cold steps and Lisa hesitated at the bottom, not knowing which corridor to choose of the three that spread from the stair base into the darkness. Donna brushed passed her and grabbed her hand roughly as she did so, pulling her towards what Lisa recognized as the White Room. She watched, puzzled, as her Mother put on a pair of dark glasses. If she had wandered why, the answer came quickly enough. Her Mother opened the door and dragged the now slightly terrified and reluctant Lisa past her and into the room. Then she flicked on the light switch. When she did so, the effect was blinding and Lisa could see nothing but white light before her eyes. She put her hands up to her face, disoriented.

"Mummy!" she screamed.

Donna, for an instant, thought better of her plan. But the moment passed as she reassured herself that this was for the best. That her child needed to be taught a valuable lesson about discipline and compliance and self restraint.

"It's alright Lisa," her voice was soft and warm, "here, come and sit next to me." Donna sat on the edge of the white bed and patted it for her daughter to join her. Lisa, peeping through gaps in her fingers, found her way there and sat down.

"Now then, listen to me. You're going to stay in here for a while. I want you to think about what you did today and why it was wrong and how you have caused me pain. Do you understand?"

"Yes Mummy. I know I was naughty, but please don't leave me in here on my own."

"Well, Lisa, this is not the first time you have been naughty, is it? And despite my having talked to you, asked you to change your ways, there doesn't seem to have been any progress, in fact, it's clear today that things are getting worse. And do you know why today you have been so much more naughty?"

Lisa looked at her and thought carefully, hoping not to get it wrong.

"Because I might have hurt myself?"

"Well, there is that. But there is something else too." Donna raised her eyebrows expectantly, but Lisa was at a loss.

"The fact you are unable to tell me speaks for itself Lisa. You simply do not know how bad you are. What you did was keep a very big secret from me. And whilst I am sure you feel very proud of yourself for hiding away in Alfred's shed and building your silly little contraption, you will never keep a secret form me again. Do you understand?"

"Yes Mummy. I'm sorry. I wanted to surprise you. I won't do it again."

"I don't like surprises. Ever. So no, you won't do it again." Donna sighed and stood up. "Now. Lie down."

Lisa lay on her back, her hands still covering her eyes from the glaring whiteness that surrounded her.

"Now, I'm sure being quiet in here will help you to think about things carefully. It will do you good. I shall be back to collect you later. Alright?"

"Yes Mummy," replied Lisa miserably.

"And another thing. This is our secret. Understand?"

"But I thought you didn't like them?" Lisa was confused again.

"I don't like *you* keeping secrets. But we have *our* secrets. And we have them so that I can protect you? Do you understand?

"Yes." Though she didn't at all.

"In return I will not tell your Father how naughty you have been. I don't want him to be as upset with you as I am. Alright?"

Lisa fleetingly thought that her Father might be more likely to laugh than be cross, but she couldn't risk it.

"Yes Mummy. Thank you."

Donna walked to the door. She looked back at her daughter lying supine on the bed and for a moment, her hand hovered over the light switch, but then it dropped and without a further word, she left the room.

What Lisa remembered about that instant when her Mother withdrew was simple. Fear. Paralysing fear. She was frightened to remove her hands from her face for fear of what might be hiding in the colourless air. As if a huge white hairy monster might be lurking in the snowy light. And she didn't dare move. The silence was deafening

34

and she expected at any moment that it would be broken by some huge beastly sound; maybe a roar or a scream. Her mind was in panic, but she had no tools to protect herself from what might be out there. She decided she had to make herself as small and quiet as possible. It took her some time to release herself from the immobilising stiffness her muscles had enforced, but eventually she was able to release them enough to turn carefully on her side and draw her knees up tight to her chest. Then she focused on breathing as slowly and quietly as she possibly could. And she counted. The way Peters had taught her to count the seconds as they played Hide and Seek. One Mississippi, two Mississippi, three Mississippi….

She had no idea how long it had taken to fall asleep but eventually she had. She was snapped awake by the door opening with huge force. Peters face suddenly loomed over her. She was clearly angry and at first Lisa recoiled.

"Angel, what has she done to you?" Peters took her hand, "come with me, Lisa, let's get you out of here."

Lisa hesitated. She desperately wanted to go, but she was frightened to without her Mother's permission.

"It's alright," Peters was aware of her predicament, "I'll speak to your Mother. Everything's going to be ok."

"You won't tell Daddy will you?"

Peters frowned, "No, no I won't tell him. It's ok."

As Lisa was led gently back up through the cellar door, through the hallway and into the welcoming warmth of the kitchen, she started to relax. Peters pulled out a stool by the breakfast bar and then sat down next to her with milk and cookies. But as they'd started to tuck in, Donna had burst through the door, filling her with a sense of alarm.

"Peters!"

Lisa had sputtered her milk and was about to climb down from the stool, when Peters patted her on the back and gave her a tissue to wipe her milk spattered face. "Stay here little one." She then rose calmly and, eyeing Donna with determination, had invited her to step outside of the room with her.

After they had closd the door behind them, Lisa ran to it and listened as hard as she could to the ensuing row. Her Mother got the first words in. It was the upset and angry voice. Lisa thought of it like a bird shrieking.

"What the hell do you think your doing with my daughter?"

"I might ask you the same thing." Peters was calm.

"Except she's my daughter not yours."

"Yes, if she *was* my daughter I could never treat her with such cruelty."

Lisa heard a slap. Then silence for a few moments.

"I should fire you for your insolence."

"Except you can't."

"Try me."

"I am employed by your husband's estate. And besides, what would you do without me? Apart from me, Only Alfred has been able to survive the madness here."

"Then why do you stay? Why don't you just leave?"

"Because of her. And believe me, if I thought I could leave with her, I would be gone in an instant."

"How dare you!" It was a scream and Lisa heard scuffling.

"Don't raise your hand to me again Donna, or so help me God, I will respond and you won't know what's hit you!"

"You bitch!" Her Mother sounded beside herself.

"And if I catch you locking her in that room again, I will let him know."

More silence.

"He would never believe you."

"Yes. He would."

Silence again.

"But she's my daughter! She's mine! I can do what I like with her."

"She's a child. A beautiful, spirited child. I'm not going to discuss this any further with you. I suggest you go and calm down. I'll prepare a picnic and take Lisa out in the gardens. When we get back, I'll bring tea to the conservatory for the two of you."

Stillness filled the air once more. And then her Mother gave in.

"Tea and some tiramisu. I want tiramisu." Lisa heard the clacking of her Mother's heels. She had obviously decided to walk away. After she had had the last word, obviously. Lisa ran back to her stool, settling herself just as Peters came back in through the door.

36

"Ok..." Peters sighed as she headed for the fridge, "how about a picnic, Angel? Shall we have sandwiches by the pond?"

Lisa looked lovingly at her hero and smiled, "yes please. And can we try and rescue my go-kart?"

Peters smiled at her tenacity, "we'll speak to Alfred."

And so she was saved from the White Room. At least for the time being. Only a darker turn of events would change that.

Chapter 8

Breakfast would be served in less than an hour and her 28th Birthday celebrations would begin. Celebrations chosen and dictated by her Mother. As always. The day's events would probably contain grand gestures, excessive generosity and high emotion, but little of it would be about her. As she stood now in her bathroom looking at herself in the mirror, Lisa took a bunch of her long blonde hair and wound it round her fingers thinking ironically how her golden locks had been a matter of pride to her Father, who loved it and said it made her look like an angel, whilst her Mother always expressed her distaste for it because it was in contrast to her own dark looks. How could her hair be the subject of such emotional anguish and turmoil? It was what she was born with, a part of her? As she stood and looked at it in the mirror now, she shook her head, dismayed that she had allowed whatever issue they both had with it affect her own ability to accept herself. When she was little, she had always had it short, a boyish crop that she'd been happy with, not least because its practicality allowed her to play and adventure without having to think about how she should wear it to stop it getting in her way. She'd grown it in an attempt to please both her Mother and her Father. He, because the longer it was the more he called her his Angel. Her, because at least growing the wretched stuff meant she looked more feminine. She thought now about her Mother and the prospect of spending the entire day doing things she did not wish to do and receiving gifts she had no interest in; gifts her Mother bought her because she *should* like them, not because she did. She thought back over the years at the items she had had to pretend to be delighted by; there were the pony years of course. Not just the animals but all the stuff she had to have to go with them. The only things she had appreciated were the boots, she loved to go tramping in the mud which annoyed the hell out of her Mother. Then there was the jewelry, designer earrings and necklaces, clothes; oh my god, the dresses, horrendous frou frou monstrosities that cost the earth and looked dreadful on her. Then last year she had received a luxury break which at first sounded promising - but then she had opened the ribboned envelope to read that she was to have a pamper weekend -

with her Mother. It had been like purgatory. She laughed and shook her head as she looked at her blonde tresses. "Let's give her a gift this year, shall we?" she said to her reflection. Impulsively, she opened the drawer and took out her special cutting scissors, hesitating for no more than a moment before starting to hack great chunks of hair off. As she sliced through the fine strands, her smile grew and a sense of release flooded through her. She cut and cut, mesmerised as she watched it fall to the floor, feeling elated. Then, having shawn it back to resemble the short boyish style she'd had years ago, she decided to add an even greater streak of defiance. Grabbing her electric shaver, she bent closer to the glass and buzzed a tidy line above each of her ears. Pleased, she turned from side to side and nodded appreciatively at herself. Finally, she scooped up the hair from the floor and went back into the bedroom. She grabbed her jewelry box, emptied its contents into the drawer of her bedside cabinet and put the hair she had cut inside it. She looked at her watch. Almost time for breakfast, which she now felt she was going to enjoy. Clutching the box, she lay back and shut her eyes, knowing that what she had done would break Donna's heart. As she thought about how her Mother was going to react, her mind started drifting back to the circumstances that had started the chain of events that would break her own heart.

Life at the manor was a dramatic split between day and night, between light and dark. Lisa's exposure to the evening and nighttime activity was gradual. As a little one, her bedtime was relatively early, her day was made up of breakfast, lessons, lunch, lessons, playtime, bedtime. The simple repeating pattern of childhood. She couldn't recall having left the manor grounds once, but then she had everything she needed within its confines. As she grew older and entered her teens, her bedtime became later and she started to be more aware of the way the manor changed after dark. It was as if it came alive in a very different way. It was always full of people after eight. Sometimes small groups, sometimes larger and quite frequently huge parties when the rooms and the main hallway would be bursting with revelers, roaring with song and dance and activities. She became aware over time that there was always plenty of drink available from the family brewery; that the parties centered around the alcohol.

Lisa was mainly left to her own devices, which meant all this went on around her as she played her games and kept herself busy. She would run between the dancing bodies at full tilt, dashing between her den, the kitchen and her bedroom. The party goers and visitors would sometimes acknowledge her with a pat on the head or a greeting, but for the most part she was barely aware of them, nor they her. She was much too focused on her own stuff. So what she absorbed became what for her was the normal course of life. Occasionally she would open a door and see things she thought she might not have been supposed to, people in rooms dressed in types of clothing she didn't see during the day, many people sharing beds, lots of drink and smoking. And sometimes she would be gently told to go and find something to play with and a door would be closed in her face. All in all, though, it was fun and everyone seemed very happy. But then one evening when she was thirteen, she saw something that deeply disturbed her and led to another catastrophic incident with her Mother - *and* her Father.

The party had started about nine o'clock, with guests arriving in a steady stream. Lisa had been testing some new train track for her model railway in the hallway and her Mother had told her to put it away so that the guests wouldn't trip over it. She was disappointed. Her Father had bought her a new electronic controller from his trip to LA and she was excited about exploring its capabilities, so she dragged her feet and played on for a while, hoping her Mother wouldn't notice. She still hadn't learnt. Guests started filing in. Lisa was largely oblivious, but she had clocked that the clothing was rather different this time. Lots of black shiny clothes and many were carrying riding crops, or at least similar to that, she recognised them from her disastrous efforts at pony lessons. Another disappointment to her Mother. No-one seemed to mind her though, so she kept quiet and ran the various engines from her collection using her new powerful driver. She was delighted with it and having fun.

"Lisaaaa!!"

She jumped. And quickly scrambled to her feet as her Mother clacked across the parquet floor.

"Per l'amor di Dio!!!" What did I tell you? Must you disobey everything I ask of you?"

40

Lisa felt herself flush hot red as several of the guests turned round to see what was happening. She quickly started scrambling to pick up the pieces of track on the floor. Her Mother was dressed elegantly in a long black gown, tightly fitted over her voluptuous curves.

"I will be back in five minutes Lisa and I don't want to see you here. Do you understand? I want you back in your room and this evening you must stay there."

"Yes Mummy."

Lisa stacked the pieces together as Donna sashayed away, her hips swaying as she took the tiny steps forced by the confinement of her dress. Now in a state of panic, she decided she would hide the railways track nearby so that she could be as quick as possible and get out of her Mother's way. She tucked them under both her arms and, looking across, saw her Father's study door was a little ajar. Perfect. She waited for a lull in the arrivals and then dashed across the hall. With her arms full, she turned her back to the door and pushed it open, spinning round to run in. But then she stopped in her tracks, literally, as the pile of railway pieces fell to the floor and she stood in them, looking straight into the faces of her father and a woman who was bent over his desk in front of him. Neither had any clothes on and the woman had one of the riding crops in her hand.

"Get out!"

But Lisa appeared to be stuck to the floor.

"Lisa, get out!"

She had never heard her Father shout like that at her. The two of them appeared to be as frozen as she was. The woman grabbed at some pieces of paper on the desk and held them over her chest. Her Father turned round and grabbed the first thing that came to hand, which happened to be a world globe and moved backwards to create the space between him and the woman and then held the globe in front of him. He inched sideways.

"Lisa!"

She looked at the woman. She seemed familiar, but she couldn't remember where from. Then she looked back at her Father, but she was still unable to move as her mind was registering what was going on. Her Father stepped sideways behind the globe until he reached the small leather sofa at the far side of the room which was covered in clothes that had been thrown there carelessly. He grabbed his trousers. He hurriedly pulled them on and then strode over to her, grabbing her roughly by the shoulder and pushing her towards the door. As they reached it, her Father shoved her through it so hard that she stumbled and fell. Right at her returning Mother's feet. She peered upwards. Donna was still staring at the study door. She slowly looked down at her daughter. Her voice was low and calm.

"This is the trouble you cause when you don't do as you are told."

Lisa wasn't sure what trouble it was she had caused, but she knew that whatever it was, there were going to be consequences. Donna clicked her fingers and pointed towards the kitchen. Lisa didn't need any more encouragement. She ran as fast as she could, hurtling through the door into her place of safety, where Peters and a number of women dressed as maids in very short skirts, were placing mounds of food onto silver trays.

"Put the caviar on the large silver platter," Peters instructed one of them and then turned to see Lisa. The look on the girls face immediately caused concern.

"What's happened?"

But before Lisa could say anything, Donna burst through the door.

"Peters! A word!"

Donna indicated that Peters should follow her into the vast pantry room at the back of the kitchen. Lisa hovered, disconcerted by the several pairs of curious eyes as the maids all stared at her. She strained her ears, trying to hear and caught only a few sentences... "too young to tell her... she won't understand that... needs to know... the sooner she is introduced the better... I will do the explaining... she's thirteen... really just a child... want to be there when you do..." none of it made sense to her.

The two of them emerged together, Peters told the Maids to carry on and serve the food and then took Lisa's hand,

"come on Angel, we need to talk to you."

Peters squeezed her hand and Lisa felt a little comforted, but she was still bewildered and confused. Her mind went back to the image she had seen as she had gone through the study door, of her

Father. She didn't know what it meant. Her Mother led the way up to her bedroom, with her and Peters following. The party was in full swing, lots of people dancing very close to each other. As they passed a bedroom door on the first floor, she caught a glimpse of someone in a swing, it was swaying back and forth above the bed and the woman was laughing. Lisa wished she was on the swing. They seemed to be having fun. Then they arrived to her room and her Mother told her to sit on the bed. Peters winked and nodded at her to go ahead. She sat down. Her Mother paced.

"What you saw earlier. Your Father." She paced again. Lisa wondered if she was meant to reply.

"He was sharing himself with someone. A prostitute."

Peters gasped.

"Donna I..."

"Be quiet Peters. If you interrupt again, you will have to leave the room."

Peters sat by Lisa and clasped her hand in both of hers. Donna continued.

"Your Father loves me. And he loves you. And he loves many other people. He likes to share his love. In many ways." Donna paced some more. "I'm sorry you saw it tonight."

Lisa catapulted herself off the bed and ran to her Mother, throwing her arms around her and sobbing. She had never heard an apology from her before. Donna started to fold her arms around her, and her face softened, but then she dropped them back down by her sides and her expression hardened again.

"Next time I ask you to do something, I want you to do it. Do you understand?"

"Yes. I'm sorry."

She withdrew awkwardly, desperately disappointed that her Mother had still not been able to hug her.

"Peters, get Lisa some late supper. Something sweet. And some milk." She turned back to her daughter, "Now it's time for bed, stay in your room tonight Lisa."

Donna nodded at Peters to follow her and they both left the room. Lisa thought about what she had seen and what her Mother had said. She was still confused, but there was one thing she had been glad about at least; her Father was receiving some love.

      The incident was not mentioned again and Lisa made sure from then on to do what her Mother said. But after that night, things changed. She did not see her Father again for over three months. Her Mother told her he was filming, but Lisa found that strange since he always told her about his projects and he hadn't mentioned anything to her. And when he did finally return, he was different. He was cold and distant with her and often avoided her company altogether. So she tried even harder to be good. She no longer played in the hall when they had parties and she spent more time with her Mother. She studied as hard as she could to get good grades, but whatever she did, nothing seemed to be enough to make either of her parents pay attention to her. Donna was different too, she spent more time on her own projects and even less time with her Father than she had before. She was more focused on the 'family business' that had grown out of the work her Father had started in the brewery and she had a crowd of friends she spent a lot of time with, starting a yoga group. They met on the lawn and didn't wear any clothes. Her Mother said it was 'liberating'. Bizarrely to Lisa, even though her parents were apart more, the parties and gatherings at the Manor grew in frequency, there were visitors more or less daily. And then, a few moths later, they stopped. Lisa wasn't sure how long it was before she noticed the silence, four or five days? Maybe a little longer? And her Father was absent again. As she remembered it now, she woke up one morning and felt the quiet, which in one way was welcome, but in another was unsettling. She suddenly felt compelled to find out why. She'd dashed down the stairs to the kitchen to find Peters, in the kitchen as usual. Running up to her, a little breathless from flying down the stairs at a rate of knots, she was all ready to find out what was happening. But as she looked at her, she thought she might not want to know.

      "Good morning Angel. Where's the fire today?"
Lisa had fiddled with some cutlery on the table.
"Cat got your tongue?"
"No, sorry, good morning. Ummm..."
"Yes?"

"I was wondering something."

"Yes?"

"Why no-one's been coming to visit. It's been really quiet for the last few days."

Peters shifted uncomfortably.

"No."

"Why?"

"It's probably something you should talk to your Mother about."

"I don't want to talk to her about it. I want to talk to you."

Peters turned to the table and busied herself slicing some bread.

"Has something happened?" For some reason the hairs went up on Lisa's neck and she suddenly felt a wave of fear, without having any idea why.

"Things are always happening here," said Peters, turning back to look at her. Lisa didn't like what she saw in Peters eyes. Sadness?

"Things have been difficult. Between you Mother and Father. For a long time now." Peters took Lisa's hand in hers, but Lisa shook her off, suddenly knowing that she didn't want to hear what Peters had to say. "Sometimes things between people go wrong and..."

"No. No, I don't want to know!"

Lisa turned and ran from the kitchen out to the hall. When she got there she stopped. She stood and listened. Silence. Something made her turn and look towards her Father's study. She hadn't dare enter it since the incident, but now something propelled her towards the door. She stopped in front of it and knocked. No answer. She knocked again. Still nothing. One final try, this time harder. No sound. She warpped her fingers round the handle, then hesitated, her heart in her mouth. Should she risk it? She took a deep breath, turned it, then pushed. The door opened and her heart sank as she looked around the room, instantly knowing that all the things that her Father treasured in there had gone. His leather writing set was not on the heavy wooden desk, the chess set that was always on the corner of the table with a part played game had disappeared, his collection of antique cameras was no longer arranged in neat rows on the bookshelves. And the globe. The globe had gone too. With tears running down her cheeks and a feeling of panic clutching at her chest, she ran from the room and out into the

45

conservatory, where her Mother was sitting cross legged on a yoga mat.

"Where's Daddy?"

Donna did not move.

"Where's Daddy?" she shouted it this time.

"I'm meditating."

"Where's Daddy?" It was a piercing scream, so emotionally charged that even Donna's generally impenetrable walls were shattered. She jumped up and rushed to her child folding her in her arms for the first time since she had been a baby. Lisa instantly felt the Mother comfort she craved but never received, she crumpled in Donna's embrace and cried; great heaving sobs, waiting for the words she already knew.

"He's gone, my darling. I'm sorry." She held her daughter until the weeping subsided. And then she let go. And that was it. The moment that Lisa first understood heartbreak, the comfort lasted a few minutes and then it too was lost.

"He doesn't love us any more. He's moved back to LA." Donna sat back on the yoga mat and resumed Lotus. "It's just you and me now."

"No!" Lisa stamped her foot, wiping her face with her arm and willing herself to stop the tears, "Daddy loves me. I'm his Angel. He wouldn't do that."

"Well. Maybe his Angel has fallen. Maybe her insistence on disobeying rules and having to poke her nose into what's going on where she's not welcome has finally driven him away. Now he loves someone else."

Lisa fell silent for a few minutes.

"You're a liar!" she stamped her feet again, "he loves me."

"No! And that's enough!" Donna rang the small bell she kept by her at all times.

Lisa's anger boiled as she watched her Mother sitting emotionless on her mat. She scanned the room and eyed Donna's fine art deco figurines. Running full pelt, she started across the carpet, like a heat seeking missile, focused entirely on her target. Donna, realising her intent, tried desperately to catch her, lunging across as she dashed by, but she didn't stand a chance. Nimbly, Lisa dodged her outstretched arm and reaching the cabinet, ran along the length of it, sweeping everything onto the floor. The sound of crashing china filled the room as Peters came through the door in response to Donna's summoning bell.

"Dear Lord!" Peters surveyed the mayhem.

Lisa, her face now contorted with rage, ran to a coffee table in the corner, home to a grand Chinese lamp.

"No!" Donna shrieked as the exquisite piece flew through the air and smashed against the wall, "tu piccola bastardo! Peters, grab her!"

Peters walked calmly towards Lisa, who was now surveying the room for more objects to destroy, "Lisa, come on, I know you're upset, but.."

Lisa looked Peters in the eyes and then collapsed into a heap on the floor. Peters knelt down and took the sobbing girl into her arms.

"He doesn't love me any more."

"Yes he does." Peters frowned up at Donna, who turned her head away and stared out of the window.

"He doesn't. He left me."

"He does love you. He didn't leave because of you."

Lisa let out a piercing scream and Peters held her tighter. Donna finally spoke. Her voice was gentle.

"I think you should prepare the Quiet Room."

"Noooooooooo..." Lisa sobbed and gripped Peters.

"Donna no, she's upset."

"She's hysterical. It's not normal."

"It's perfectly normal under the circumstances."

"It's not. She's not. She needs to learn some discipline."

"That's not the way," Peters protested.

"It's my way. And if you don't wish to do things my way, you can leave."

A stony silence hung in the air.

"You can't leave too, you can't! You're all I have!" The emotion in Lisa's voice ripped through Peters heart and threw another layer of steel around Donna's, who looked on filled with jealousy and dismay as her daughter expressed her singular devotion to a woman she regarded as her servant.

"I'm not going anywhere Angel," she said, stroking her hair. She looked up at Donna and nodded, "I'll take her."

"You're on thin ice. Don't try anything."

"Just let me take her, she'll be calmer."

Donna looked at her miserable daughter dispassionately. "Your Father has gone, now you will have to do as you are told, there's no escape. Poor fallen Angel."

Peters gently helped Lisa to her feet and put her arm round her shoulder, leading her from the room. As they reached the door, Donna spoke again.

"Just so you know, there's a CCTV camera in there now. So I'll say it again. Don't try anything." Peters just looked at her and shook her head sadly. Donna offered a charming smile.

Lisa opened her eyes and stared for a few moments at the ceiling, remembering particularly those few minutes in the kitchen. Peters hadn't seen her pick up the little pair of kitchen scissors that had been left on the worktop. She held up her arm above her head as she lay there now and looked at them. They had become her friend, her special cutting scissors. She had tucked them into the top of her jeans and then let Peters take her by the hand and lead her to the White Room. It had been a long time, but the hairs went up on the back of her neck as they descended into the cellar, she had not forgotten the feelings that had been evoked the first time she had been there. Peters had promised her that she would talk to her about her Father when she came out, but something had changed in Lisa's head. Not that she felt anger towards her Father, quite the reverse, but she didn't want to know any more about why. Looking back now, she recognised it as a pivotal moment, when the pain of knowing that she might have been responsible for his departure had flipped a switch in her head. She had felt like she no longer cared about anything, as if the switch had activated a metal cage that had snapped shut around her heart. She would no longer care about anything or anyone, with the exception of her hero, who had stood by her as she had lain down on the bed and shut her eyes.

"I'll be back for you as soon as I can, I promise."

"I know."

"Try to sleep."

As Peters left the room, Lisa had stared up at the CCTV camera, a determined, belligerent look on her face. Then she had pulled the top white sheet up over her head and turned on her side. Beneath the cotton coverlet, she had taken the scissors carefully from her jeans. She looked at a wound in the crook of her arm she had received climbing a tree a couple of days before. There was a momentary struggle as one half of her mind suggested she go ahead, whilst the other half told her not to do it. But rational thought quickly caved in to the need to release herself from the mental anguish she was in, and she plunged the sharp point of the scissors into the wound. As she felt blood flow, she experienced an instant sense of relief. The pain in her body gave her mind something to focus on other than the emotional trauma of her loss - and it had felt good. Her Mother had seen the blood as it had seeped onto the white material, a stark pool of red on the immaculate white canvas. A few minutes later, Peters had come to rescue her. Donna, of course was furious. They'd called the Doctor, Taylor, who had stitched the wound and dressed it. She remembered her Mother asking the Doctor how to deal with it. The words were still etched on her like so many others from these incidents. The Doctor, far from offering a caring sense of sympathy for her plight, had been as cold and callous as her Mother.

"Give her these, they're sedatives. And then consider using restraints. That will stop her."

She looked now at the scar on her arm, one she had re-opened many times over the years. Then she looked at the scissors and thanked them, for being there for her when she had needed that release, but now she knew she no longer required them. Cutting her hair had been their last task, it was time to say goodbye.

Chapter 10

It was a quiet day in the post office and Theresa finally had some thinking time to consider the disturbing events that were going on around her. Events that made her feel a lack of control. And when she didn't feel tightly in control, it put her emotions out of kilter in every respect. It made her irritable and snappy - Roy had already had the sharp end of her tongue that morning over his crusty rolls and the state of his Stinking Bishop. Both the bread and the cheese counters were an important part of their revenue and she couldn't be doing with him letting goods go off. Doug's bout of petulance over the cream was a wake up call. A lesson. "You see what happens when you lose control even just a little? Your pot of cream became a mini crisis. I need to you to be more attentive Roy. And more creative. Put your thinking cap on. There are any number of solutions to that particular dilemma. You could have added lemon to the cream and called it Sour. You might even be able to sell some tortillas with it."

"We don't sell tortillas," he had said, frustratingly.

"That's not the point!" she had roared, "the point is to think about it and come up with a solution that won't cause trouble! And that won't mean we have to waste goods!"

Roy had made no further response. He knew when he was in a no win with Theresa. She watched him now as he sought to redeem himself by examining the produce for tell tale signs; hard loaves and over ripe cheese. As he prodded and sniffed, her mind turned back to the subject of Lisa. She knew there was something wrong. Her dissention was far from normal and it implied a level of independence that simply didn't stack up. Under typical circumstances her compulsion would never have allowed such behaviour. So to Theresa it sounded an alarm bell. There was an obvious explanation, but she wondered how that could possibly be, given Donna's total commitment to The Club. She would need to investigate further. Perhaps it was time to call in Nathan and look at some CCTV footage. Maybe then she would get a better sense of what was happening - and there was always the possibility of a little more surveillance. She wrote herself a note and resolved to set some wheels in motion later that day.

Then there was the much larger issue with Grace Edwards. Theresa sighed. The implications of that were so severe that she had deliberately pushed it to the back of her mind. Sorting out the mess that was about to create was going to be a major task. One that would require an enormous amount of collaboration within the village. The expression 'it doesn't bear thinking about' was wholly accurate, she almost could not bear to face the challenge it represented. She was confounded as to how Grace had managed to sell her property to someone outside the village in the first place. How could that possibly happen without anyone knowing? It couldn't, she concluded. So someone must have known - and kept it quiet. The upshot was that they would soon have new residents in the village who were Outsiders. That hadn't happened for over a decade. Their close knit community was about to be invaded. Theresa felt a knot form in her stomach. She regarded Roy again, who was struggling to scrape a piece of runny brie off his board, and wondered about him. She hated the thought that ran through her head, but he was, after all, one of Grace's confidantes. It seemed incomprehensible that he wouldn't have known.

"That looks a bit sticky? Do you need some help?"

"No. I've got it. Going to chop it up and add it to a Pizza top."

Theresa nodded at him and he looked pleased with himself. She felt herself melt at his cuteness. He always managed to get to her heart one way or another.

"Smart thinking my man," she said kindly.

He winked at her, "no flies on me today. Or my dairy."

Theresa smiled. She loved it when he did as he was told. She looked at her watch, wondering if she might be able to sneak out for an hour and head up to the manor to see Donna. She really needed to get a grip on what was happening. She stuck the cardboard sign saying 'Closed. Come Back Later' on her little counter and picked up her bag before walking towards the door.

"Roy, I'm going out, there's something I need to deal with urgently. Man the shop ok?"

"Right you are," he didn't bother to ask where she was going, she had that look that said 'don't ask if you don't want to get my goat'. And the last thing he needed was Theresa's goat.

"I'll be back in an hour."

51

Roy looked at his runny brie and sighed. There was trouble afoot.

When Lisa entered the dining room for breakfast, her Mother was waiting for her with a huge smile on her face as usual. Moving towards her with a glass of mimosa in her hand, the happiness had faded very quickly.

"What on earth have you done to your hair?"

Lisa kept her head high, "do you like it? I cut it myself. I love it."

"It's gruesome." Her Mother sighed a deep sigh, "I suppose you had to do it today didn't you? To ruin my day?"

"Don't you mean ruin my day?"

"Don't start your nonsense Lisa, not today. It's your birthday and you're not going to spoil it for me." Donna plastered her smile back on, "so darling, many happy returns, twenty-eight years young!" Donna handed her the glass.

"No thank you Mother," Lisa turned to Peters who was standing in the corner of the room looking on with quiet amusement, "could I have a plain orange juice?"

"Of course you can Angel."

Donna took a deep breath, "So! Take your seat, I have surprises!"

Lisa sat at the end of the long table.

"I'm not wearing the Princess crown."

Donna sighed again,

"Fine. Now. Your first surprise before we eat." Donna clicked her fingers at Peters, who raised a sardonic eyebrow at Lisa and placed a box in front of her with a flourish. Lisa looked at it disinterestedly and lazily pulled the ribbon on the box before removing the lid. She glanced up at her Mother, who was grinning from ear to ear.

"Isn't it divine?"

"It's a dress."

Donna clapped her hands, "just wait until you find out what it's for!" Lisa couldn't imagine there was anything it could be for that she might be interested in. And this year, she wasn't even going to try to lie about how she felt about the useless gifts her Mother gave her.

"I don't like dresses."

Donna ignored her. "Peters serve breakfast would you?"

Three courses of luxury breakfast followed, Lisa was largely silent, insolent and like a storm brewing, her mood darkened as the time dragged by. Her Mother, by contrast, kept up a constant stream of dialogue. About nothing, or at least nothing that any longer passed for anything interesting to Lisa. It swept past her. She ate little of the splendid array of food that was put in front of her. But if her Mother noticed her behaviour, she wasn't about to show it. After the coffee cups had finally been cleared away, her Mother walked grandly down the table and placed an envelope in front of her.

"Happy Birthday darling."

Lisa picked it up and opened it slowly, indifferently. It contained a ticket that had been drawn up specially. It told her that she would be going to Rome. She would be spending 4 days there touring the city. She would be given special access to the Vatican. And she would be going to the opera. Which was what the dress was for. She should have been filled with joy. Her first visit outside the UK since they had arrived in the village, but this very special event would be in the company of her Mother. Torture in Rome.

"Thank you." She said it flatly and closed the envelope.

Her Mother was just about to respond when a knock at the door interrupted her.

"Come!" she barked.

Alfred entered the room, "beg you pardon ma'am, but Theresa Jones is here to see you, says it's urgent."

Donna looked at her watch and then her daughter, "Alright Alfred, I'll be there in a couple of minutes." Lisa could see she was conflicted, her obnoxious attitude finally having an impact. "Why can't you just be happy for the day? Why do you have to ruin it? I've put a lot of effort into this, as I always do on your birthday, why can't you enjoy it? Be grateful, show some appreciation? Is that really too much to ask when you are being spoilt rotten?"

"Because my birthdays are not about me, they're about you. Because I don't want your generosity when the gifts are what you think I should have not what I actually might like or enjoy. Because your happiness and excitement is a facade... should I continue?"

"I'm going to speak to Theresa, perhaps you could go to your room for a while and come back down with a smile on your face."

"A false one like yours?"

"I frankly don't care what kind of smile it is, as long as you put one on. In the same way I have had to despite circumstances. I think you will find that no matter what has been going on around me, on your birthday I have also stepped up and made sure you would see nothing but smiles and happiness for your special day. I would be grateful if today you would do me the same courtesy."

Donna marched from the room, leaving Lisa feeling small. As always. She tapped the jewelry box she had meant to give her Mother as a gift, her golden locks curled inside as a pointed memento of her only attempt at the femininity she had made. It seemed now a meaningless gesture and she felt grateful that she hadn't had the chance to present it. What was the point of trying to play the same games her Mother did? She rose wearily and went back up the stairs, her resolve to own the day and do as she pleased, now somewhat dented. She lay on the bed again and thought back to her eighteenth birthday.

After her father left, Lisa's life had become much more restricted. There was less opportunity for her to spend time in her adored gardens. She was allowed to play tennis and a golf instructor was shipped in to teach her the game on a special five-hole course that had been landscaped in the grounds. She was forced back onto horses and her Mother tried to get her into equestrian events, but a few broken bones later, that was abandoned. Her tutoring continued, she took her exams as required and largely excelled. She spent a lot of time with her Mother, read, learned the piano. She took ballroom dancing lessons and for a brief, unsuccessful time, ballet. She still rarely left the boundaries of the manor. Then, on her Eighteenth birthday, Lisa's life took another twist. Her Mother lavished gifts on her, they had a balloon ride over the village at dawn, she landed to find a new thoroughbred in the stable waiting for her and a beautiful white evening dress with an exquisite diamond necklace and earrings. Despite Lisa's normal insistence that dresses were not for her, this one had a simple elegance that actually appealed to her. For once she felt she would enjoy wearing it. Then, in the evening, her Mother invited her to take drinks with her for the first time.

Donna drank cocktails every day at six, it was a ritual. The family brewing business was a matter of huge pride and Lisa was aware it was a significant generator of wealth. Her father had loved the brewery and spent much of his time working on the secret recipes for the beer and the Gin they made there. The occasional times she had been allowed to go with him, she had loved it too. It was like a magical kingdom. The old building was like a castle to her, with it's strange turrets on the top and its moat, now dry. Lisa had imagined it had a past life as a home for a King and Queen, defended against invaders by brave knights who shot bows and arrows through its tiny windows. She longed to run around its corridors pretending to be one of those knights, but she had been strictly forbidden to explore. She'd never been allowed to try any of the products and frankly had little interest in them. It was the romance of the building itself that fascinated and engaged her.

Peters served them and on this day, she arrived with a tray, on which two glasses sat. One she recognised as her Mother's usual drink, a Voluptuous Venus, glowing red in its crystal martini glass, fresh raspberries floating on its surface. The other was a vibrant green, finished with what looked like a herb. Peters handed Donna a piece of card and as she glanced across at her, Lisa had sensed that Peters did not altogether approve.

"So. Darling. Your first taste of the family Gin. I'm very excited for you. The brewery has made a special cocktail for you. It will be your cocktail from now on."

Her Mother handed her the card and Lisa read its content and looked up at her Mother, tears forming in her eyes. Her drink was called Fallen Angel.

Her Mother watched her intently as she handed her the glass. Lisa wanted to weep. Nonetheless she took it and her Mother raised the toast.

"To your coming of age." Lisa dutifully raised her glass and took a sip. Sweet, minty, strong and with a tang. Her head swam. And then something strange happened. All of a sudden her sadness was replaced with an incredible euphoria, but in a bizarre way, as if one part of her was reveling in ecstasy and another, smaller, less influential part was questioning how that could be. She remembered an inexplicable rush of something positive, but indefinable, towards her Mother. She wanted to describe it as a feeling, but somehow couldn't. Donna rasied a toast.

"To you my darling. Now your life will change. Just you wait and see, everything is going to feel so much better for you."

Lisa remembered that moment so well. She remembered the way her face had stretched into a smile that was a mirror of her Mothers. Wide, brilliant, glowing - and somehow completely devoid of feeling. Numb.

Every day after that, she joined her Mother for cocktails. Always at six. Always a Voluptuous Venus for her Mother and a Fallen Angel for her. Always the same feeling of euphoria. The flood of something rushing through her body that she couldn't describe with any clarity. About a week later, as they sipped their cocktails, her Mother had broached the subject of life in the village.

"You know we live in a very special place Lisa."

"Yes."

"We're privileged. And we're lucky to have the kind of freedom we have, to live the way we want to live, without the restrictions that society normally oppresses us with. We are able to share, in our own little world, the kind of openness that most people only ever dream of. Your Father created this world for us. It is his legacy. He may not be here right now, but this place contains his spirit."

Lisa sipped her drink and thought about what her Mother was saying, she wasn't sure she entirely understood. Her own life felt restricted by the rules of her Mother, but she agreed about her Father's spirit. She could still feel his presence in the manor house, in the special places and secrets they shared and for that she felt a sense of gratitude - and perhaps her Mother deserved some of that gratitude for keeping that alive for her. She decided to hang on to the last few words and the hope that 'he may not be here right now' meant that he might be here again in the future.

"Do you remember the night you saw your Father in the study?"

"Yes." Lisa frowned, it was a memory she frequently tried to force from her mind, it made her feel somehow responsible for driving her Father away.

"Do you remember what I told you about the woman he was sharing his time with?"

"Yes."

"She made your Father happy. There were others who made him happy too. That kind of openness and sharing is one of the reasons we have such a positive community here. We all share in and enjoy each others happiness. You want to be happy don't you and to make others happy in the way that your Father was happy?"

"I suppose so, yes."

"Good. Then we're going to have a party at the weekend. Do you remember all the parties we used to have?"

"Yes."

"We'll have a party just like that. That's what your new dress is for. It's a kind of coming out ball, it's a celebration for you."

Lisa nodded, she had no feelings one way or the other about the party, she felt a kind of happy numbness that felt like floating. That life could wash over and around her and whatever it brought she would be ok. Her Mother continued.

"You know I love you, don't you?"

Lisa listened to her Mothers words, the first ever expression of love from her. They were delivered with a kind of blankness that echoed through her core. She felt nothing. Void. So that was love. That was how love felt. Like numbness, like nothing.

"Yes," she replied, with the same emptiness.

"Good. And I only want the best for you. To keep you safe. To protect you."

"Yes." Lisa followed her Mothers eyes out across the Manor lawns where the sun stretched the shadows of a small group of naked women performing a Sun Salutation in its evening glow. They each settled into their own thoughts, watching the group in silence.

In a back corner of the room, Peters stood in the shadows listening to the two women. Her heart was breaking at the innocence she heard and saw in Lisa. Peters was acutely aware that the life she was in, the circumstances of her surroundings, were the only thing she knew. That the tender, broken soul inside was trapped by a truth it could not break away from or even know for the illusion of reality that it was. That her life for now was an echo of her own Mother's dysfunctional journey. Like Donna, her very essence was being incarcerated by a reality that had been manufactured by her Father. A tear tumbled down her cheek and she took an oath to her soul that whatever happened, she would be there for Lisa and that some day, she would help set her free.

Ten years ago, the party had been Lisa's first taste of the 'freedom' the community had to offer. When she looked back now with the benefit of clarity, she was able to see it for what it was. The trap that had been set for her since she was five years old.

The day had started with her Mother fussing around her, making sure she would be ready for the evening. Washed, styled, dressed. She hadn't been allowed to leave her room until the party started and a parade of women had helped her with her 'look', her blonde hair piled on her head with ringlets teased into a tumbling blonde cascade, manicured, pedicured and with her first mask of make up applied, she felt like a dress up doll. Looking in the mirror at the finished item, she wondered who it was staring back at her from the reflection. At 9pm her Mother and Peters had joined her in her room for their cocktails; her Mother was dressed in an elegant black ball gown, tightly fitting her voluptuous curves down to her calves and then flowing back into a sea of material that formed a train that she hooked up over her arm as she walked. Lisa remembered Donna's excitement as she had appraised her daughter.

"Bellisima! E semplicemente bella." Her Mother had been beside herself with joy. "Questa e mia figlia" she had talked to herself as if Lisa had not been there, "finalmente. Ora tu sei la mia angelica."

Lisa glanced at Peters, who offered a sympathetic look. Then she looked in the mirror again. This was the angelic daughter her Mother had wanted. Well, this Fallen Angel was what she would now have. Lisa felt a cold rush run through her. Her Mother then gave her the last piece of her outfit. A white-winged feather and lace Venetian eye mask. The masquerade was complete.

A few minutes later, the two of them had walked out to the top of the grand curving staircase to be presented to the excited throng of partygoers now gathered in the hall below. A gong sounded. Lisa looked at the sea of masked guests dressed either completely in black or totally white. The room fell silent.

"Ladies and Gentleman, welcome. Tonight we celebrate my beautiful daughter Lisa's Eighteenth Birthday. Her coming of Age. She joins us in the name of her Father, she will walk his path. All that we see is ours to share. All that we are, we can be with freedom and joy. We embrace our Angels and our Demons and tonight will honour our darkness and our light." A waiter stepped forward with two shot glasses, which they each took. Her Mother continued, "to the future of the Danforths and our community. To our daughter. To The Club."

The gathered group all raised their glasses and echoed Donna's last words.

"The Club"

The shots were downed, Lisa followed suit, tasting the bittersweet fruit and spices of the neat Gin as it slipped down the back of her throat. The slightly burning effect was darkly delicious, it sent her mind flying and her body felt like a floating vessel and as Donna indicated that she should walk down the stairs on one side, whilst she would take the other, it seemed as if she was on air, her feet gliding effortlessly. Their descent was as dramatic as Lisa's was to be that night, as they merged into the welcoming group of revelers.

Her memory of the events from then on was hazy but she was able to look back now and know why she had made her subsequent choices about her life in the village. Firstly, there had been the overwhelming sensation of belonging. The party goers had been welcoming and warm, she had felt like she was being folded into their collective arms. There really was a sense of joy and freedom in the room, perhaps the one her Mother had alluded to. For that night, there was no sense of oppression, there were no rules, just people enjoying each other, laughing, having fun. She had danced in a way she had never danced before, with no sense of restriction, with no concern for how she looked or whether the way she moved might be less than perfect, whether the steps she took were the right ones. Because no-one judged, no-one cared. She knew now that part of the secret of that inhibition had lain in the masks. No-one could be identified, they did not need to know who they were, they had their identity, but it was hidden by an outward appearance that concealed their very human fears. Comparison, competition, correctness; none of these were necessary. And the anonymity had resulted in a free expression of attraction; her first experience of physical intimacy had been anonymous. The result had been a type of happiness that was as divorced from connection as it was possible to be. And yet there had been a type of fulfillment in that she was able to recognise. Because she had seen it years before. In her Father's eyes. And her Mother had told her this was love, this was happiness. In the moment, in the time that she knew this as love, her body had flooded her with the chemicals that were to become her obsession, her addiction, her connection with the one person in her life she had felt a true and meaningful love for. Her Father.

At breakfast the following morning her Mother had been subdued. They ate mostly in silence. For her own part, Lisa felt a sense of satisfaction, that she had been embraced by a group of people and experienced a sense of belonging that had been missing from her life. Was it family? She didn't know. It was hard to define. More in the sense of how she felt than the feeling she had created in others. She knew she had shared and given happiness, that others had experienced fulfilment as a result of what she had given. What she had received had been closeness to her father. And that meant a huge amount to her.

"Did you enjoy your party?" Donna's voice had that flatness to it. Detached.

"Yes."

"You are your Father's daughter."

"Yes."

"I recognise that it matters not how I dress you, how you appear. Your essence remains the same."

"Yes."

"You must decide from here what your role will be. How you will contribute to the development of our community."

"Yes. I know. I want to share. I want to know what he felt."

60

Donna looked up at her daughter.

"You can't know that."

"I can try."

"If I allow it."

"You will allow it." Lisa was sure of this. She had become intensely aware of her Mother's pain. Of her loss. Of her need to see the echo of it in her daughter.

"I will be the happiness."

"You know what that means?"

"Yes."

"So be it. The World's oldest profession. It carries a great responsibility."

"I know."

As she prepared to go down for cocktails with her Mother, Lisa felt weary. Like she was fighting against the tide that had swept her along for so many years. She couldn't pinpoint the time at which she had acknowledged that her life was still the masquerade she had joined all those years ago. That although there was a sense of belonging, of acceptance, it came with the price of true feeling. That the 'freedom' she felt was not real, it was an illusion created by her mind's desperate need to feel something other than the pain of loss. Even if that turned out to be numbness. She knew now that she had moved from one prison of pain to another. She looked at her newly cut hair and determined there was no going back. That for her to be who she was, she must defy her Mother's control. Break free from the safety of her current existence and take a risk on believing in herself again. In her ability to stand on her own two feet. To be independent and to leave the conditioning of the past behind. She knew she had one true ally in that battle in Peters, who had stood by her in every decision she had made. And from here forward, she would need her more than ever. She also recognised her need to play smart. As the fog of the past ten years started to lift, clarity of thinking started to return and she understood that her resistance needed to be selective, that she needed to learn far more about the consequences of real freedom before she broke away from all the chains. She needed to trust that her own instincts were the best things to rely on in making the right decisions at the right time. She looked at her reflection and fist pumped. You can do this, she said to her 'self'. You're stronger than you know. She turned and headed for the door with a new resolve, descending the stairs and walking determinedly to the conservatory to meet her Mother for cocktails.

Donna was staring out of the conservatory window. There were no yoga practitioners this evening, so her contemplation must have been reflective, thought Lisa as she entered the room. She did not greet her Mother but settled herself into an ergonomic sun lounger and closed her eyes, enjoying the peace as the afternoon sun enveloped her. Precisely on time, Peters entered the room with their cocktails. Her Mother turned and regarded first Peters and then her. She swiveled in her chair and Lisa felt a sense of discomfort. Peters approached her with the tray and Lisa took her Fallen Angel. As she thanked Peters, their eyes engaged and Lisa understood that something was not right. She was aware from the corner of her eye that her Mother was watching them intently. Peters walked over to Donna and extended the tray for her to take her drink, but her Mother's stare did not divert.

"Thank you Peters, but I think I'd like to try the Fallen Angel."

Lisa hoped her reaction was imperceptible. Peters walked back towards her and took her glass. Still she felt her Mother's eyes were on her. The Fallen Angel was placed firmly in Donna's hand. Lisa held her breath as her Mother sipped. And then sipped again. A fleeting look of surprise crossed her brow.

"Very good Peters." She handed the glass back to be returned to Lisa. Peters, with her back to Donna, winked at Lisa, who exhaled just as her lungs were about to burst.

"That will be all." Donna was dismissive and Peters took the cue, making a hasty retreat. Lisa slowly and deliberately ran her fingers through the crew cut side of her new hair style. Her Mother looked at her contemplatively.

"Don't disappoint me. And don't let your Father down."

That old trick. If all else fails, mention Daddy.

"I don't intend to. I want to be the person he really wanted me to be." She chose her words carefully, "and if you'll excuse me, I'd like to change for dinner."

Donna nodded and Lisa, relieved, took her leave.

"Thank you Mother."

Heading for the door, she felt her face flush and her heart beat faster than she could have imagined. She opened it and bolted towards the kitchen, flying through into the room with such force that she skidded on the tiled floor and landed with a thud against the refrigerator.

"Steady on." Peters was the epitome of calm.

"Fuck!" Lisa let out a huge sigh, "how did you know?"

"I saw her with Theresa earlier. I knew there were alarm bells ringing. Theresa won't come near your Mother unless there are serious issues to discuss."

"Doug?"

"Yes, amongst other things. You are clearly outside her control at the moment. It points to you not drinking the Gin. She must have suspected you were no longer under its effects. Ergo, you cocktail must no longer have Gin in it. She would have known I had to be complicit. I knew she would want to test it. So I put it back in this evening, just in case. Turned out to be a good shout."

"Thank you, thank you, thank you... Oh My God, it doesn't bear thinking about. what she would have done if she'd discovered I'd stopped taking it. I'd have been trapped in the White Room forever."

Peters allowed herself a brief smile. Then became serious again. "It was never going to be easy."

"I know and I'm so grateful, really I am. But I've felt so much better. I can see clearly, think more clearly, understand more clearly." Lisa let out another deep sigh, "I know I need to do this."

"Yes. You do. We will just have to be careful. Now, talking of that, scoot off to your room before she finds you here, ok?"

Lisa nodded, "Yes." She approached Peters and kissed her cheek, "you're my hero."

Peters winked at her, "and you're mine."

Chapter 11

In the darkness of the surveillance room, Donna tapped her lip thoughtfully. She hadn't caught her daughter out, but she was aware that was down to Peters cleverness, not that she had been wrong. She picked up her phone and dialed.

"Theresa? I'm going to need to step up surveillance, send Nathan round tomorrow."

"Of course. Any progress?"

"No. But it's just a matter of time. I will take control back. On that subject, I trust you are dealing with the issue of the incomers appropriately?"

"The wheels are in motion."

"When do they arrive?"

Donna felt Theresa's hesitation.

"Tomorrow is the completion date."

"And why did you leave it so long to tell me?"

"I wanted to find out more before I concerned you with it."

"I think you know better than that."

"Perhaps I should have discussed it sooner, but on balance I don't think it would have affected the outcome in any way."

"That's for me to judge." Donna was firm.

"Of course. I apologise."

"Send Nathan first thing."

"Of course."

Donna terminated the call and swiveled her chair to stare out of the window at the full moon, shining brightly in a cloudless night sky. It felt like a metaphor. The completion of a cycle that would tomorrow start afresh. She closed her eyes and acknowledged that new beginning.

"Yes. Things are about to change here."

In the same darkness, in her own room, Lisa lay and watched the moon too. And she too was thinking about change. She closed her eyes and looked back again at her five-year-old self, running full tilt into the manor house. Only this time, she chose to see herself bathed in light. The sea of light she need to help her swim towards a new future. She knew now that the power to shape that future was in her own hands. She didn't know what it might look like yet, but she was aware that she had already taken those first critical strokes to move through the waters that surrounded her. She understood that she needed to trust in herself and the Universe to open the doors along the way. She listened. And in the silence she heard her Father's voice echo inside her as if it was her own. "No more Fallen Angel."

How to make A Fallen Angel Cocktail

1 and ½ parts Gin
2 Dashes of crème de Menthe, White
½ part lime juice
A dash of Angostura bitters

Mix all the ingredients with ice, shake and strain into a chilled cocktail glass

To find out what happens to Lisa, our Fallen Angel, it's now time for a new cocktail...

To order your ebook or paperback copy visit Amazon stores Worldwide

for more information, related products and to find out about our video trailer visit www.ginandit.tv

For more information about me
visit www.elainesturgess.com